TIDES OF OLYMPUS

TRIALS 4, 5 & 6: APOLLO, DIONYSUS &
HEPHAESTUS

ELIZA RAINE

Editors: Anna Bowles, Kyra Wilson

Cover: The Write Wrapping

APOLLO

THE IMMORTALITY TRIALS

TRIAL FOUR

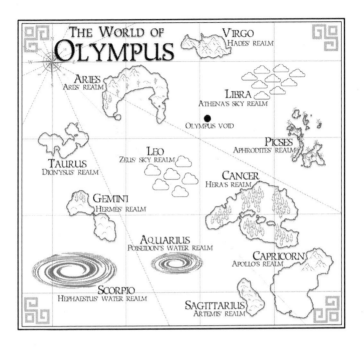

THE WORLD OF
OLYMPUS

VIRGO
HADES' REALM

ARIES
ARES' REALM

LIBRA
ATHENA'S SKY REALM

OLYMPUS VOID

PICSES
APHRODITES' REALM

TAURUS
DIONYSUS' REALM

LEO
ZEUS' SKY REALM

CANCER
HERA'S REALM

GEMINI
HERMES' REALM

AQUARIUS
POISEIDON'S WATER REALM

CAPRICORN
APOLLO'S REALM

SCORPIO
HEPHAESTUS' WATER REALM

SAGITTARIUS
ARTEMIS' REALM

1

LYSSA

'Citizens of Olympus, this is an unexpected turn of events for you!' Lyssa glared at the blond task-announcer in the flame dish, wishing she could wipe the excited smile from his face. 'Here's your next host to tell you more!' He vanished, replaced by the beaming face of the god Apollo.

'Capricorn,' she breathed. 'We're going to Capricorn.' She willed her power into the ship, directing the *Alastor* due east, as she turned to the place by the navigation wheel where Abderos usually sat. *Please let him be safe and sound when we arrive*, she prayed.

'Good day, Olympus,' said Apollo. 'The crews have probably noticed by now that they are each one member short. Sorry about that.' He smiled and winked, his white teeth flashing. 'But don't worry, you're about to have your chance to win them back – as long as you're quick enough.' Lyssa looked at Epizon, seeing his lips pinched tight together and his impatient concern a mirror of hers. 'You've each been assigned a colour, and a matching key will arrive on your ships momentarily.'

A shimmering ball appeared in the image, next to his face. It looked like it was made of metal, and an intricate pattern of vines and leaves carved into its surface was shining bright yellow. 'You will need this key if you make it through my challenges.' The image changed, his face and the sphere fading, replaced with an aerial view of a cross with a circle in the centre. 'Your crew-mates are here, heroes,' Apollo said, and the circle glowed. 'Three members of each crew will start where you see your colour.' The four ends of the cross glowed purple, white, blue and red. 'The first to reach the centre wins. And for some added incentive...' The image swirled, as though they were diving down, towards the glowing circle in the middle, then came into focus sharply. There was a cage, maybe ten feet square, with four figures inside.

Lyssa's fists clenched, her whole body tensing as she recognised Abderos, the only one not lying unconscious on the floor. He was sitting in his wheelchair, a peaceful look on his slumbering face. She watched him long enough to see his chest rise and fall, then scanned the other figures. Busiris, the gold-skinned half-giant, took up a third of the available floor space and Evadne and Theseus sprawled across each other on the remaining ground.

Theseus? Apollo had taken the *Virtus'* captain? Seconds after relief that she herself had not been taken washed through her, Lyssa felt guilty. The impotence she'd feel trapped in that cage... As she looked more closely at it, she frowned. Ice. It was made from ice.

The image wobbled and the figures stirred. The cage seemed to get smaller, the scene around it growing, and Lyssa gasped. A massive boar was running at the cage. Enormous ivory-coloured tusks curved on each side of its snout and its eyes flashed red as it powered towards the prisoners.

Lyssa held her breath as it smashed into the ice cage. The enclosure held, just quivering slightly as its inhabitants started to lift their heads.

'I'd say you have about two hours before the boar breaks into the cage. And I'm afraid he has a bad temper and a large appetite.' Apollo's face appeared and Lyssa let out her breath with a snarl. 'Oh, and it's winter in Capricorn. Very, very cold. Good luck.' The god beamed, winked again and vanished.

A LOUD METALLIC clang caused Lyssa to spin around. Nestor had picked up a sphere twice the size of her fist. The centaur held it out, and Lyssa saw that it was identical to the one that had appeared next to Apollo, except it glowed purple instead of yellow.

'Purple,' said Nestor. 'Athena's colour.'

'Is that a key?' said Len, stretching up on his hooves as best he could to look at the ball.

'If Apollo says it is, then it is. We'll be in Capricorn in less than an hour. Who's doing this with me?' Lyssa put her hands on her hips. Epizon and Nestor stepped forward in unison. Phyleus looked sideways at the navigation wheel as Len spoke.

'Captain, as much as I'd love to help Abderos, I don't think I'm your guy for physical challenges.'

'You think they'll be physical?' she asked. The satyr nodded.

'Capricorn has extreme seasons and Apollo takes the absence of the sun very seriously. In winter it will be entirely ice and snow, with little light. Any terrain will be tough.'

Lyssa cocked her head at him. 'OK. Anything else we should know?'

Len narrowed his eyes, thinking.

'Apollo is Artemis's twin.' Everyone looked at Nestor as she spoke. 'I've visited Capricorn many times in spring and fall. Apollo has a sense of humour, and he's vain. He will treat this more like a game than any of the others will. He is likely to try to show off. But if you win his respect, you'll keep it forever.'

'Right...' Lyssa said, and swallowed. 'I'm sorry, Nestor, but ice terrain does not sound ideal for a centaur.' Nestor's internal conflict showed in her face, her white-blond eyebrows drawing together.

'I suppose you are right.' She stepped backwards, her tail flicking as she looked down. Lyssa's heart went out to her. Her first chance to do something, to act on her grief and anger, and she would have to watch, helpless.

'Guess I'm up, then.' Phyleus spoke quietly. 'No rest for the wicked.' It was true, Lyssa realised. Phyleus had been involved in every Trial so far. And the last one... He'd let her go through the spikes. He'd believed she could make it. She hadn't had time to consider what he'd said about the sails turning black. To consider what may have happened if he'd not knocked her from the mast. To consider the way hatred had consumed every part of her and how terrifyingly *good* it had felt.

SHE PUSHED the thoughts from her mind. She would have Epizon by her side this time, and stopping Hercules was a secondary consideration. First and foremost they needed to get Abderos back home, safe and sound.

For his fourth labour, Hercules was told to bring back the boar that ravaged the lands
around the mountain of Erymanthus…
He found the boar looking for food and chased it into deep snow where he was able to trap
it, then bring it back with him to Mycenae.

EXCERPT FROM

The Library by Apollodorus

Written 300–100 B.C.

Paraphrased by Eliza Raine

2

EVADNE

E vadne's head was pounding and her skin was cold. A rumble and then a loud clang penetrated her consciousness and she groaned, trying to hold onto the quiet darkness behind her closed eyelids. Then she heard a shout. A man. Not Hercules.

Her eyes flew open and she sat up with a start. Someone was half-lying on top of her. She picked up an arm and tossed it off her abdomen, lip curling in disgust and confusion. Theseus. Theseus was next to her.

She looked around, panic threatening to engulf her. Another body lay on the ground next to her. It was the gold-skinned giant from the *Orion*, Busiris. And directly in front of her there was a chair with large metal wheels where a young man sat staring at her, wild-eyed.

'You're...' she struggled to remember his name.

'Abderos. I'm from the *Alastor*. There's—' He was cut off by another rumble and rattling clang. Abderos flinched, gripping the wheels of his chair. Evadne whipped her head round, gasping as she saw a boar taller than she was smash into clear glass that was surrounding them. The glass shook but held. She eased her way to her feet as the boar began backing up, its outline shimmering and warping through the glass. She touched it hesitantly and snatched her fingers back when the cold bit into her skin. Ice, not glass.

She turned slowly around on the spot. The ice enclosed them completely, barely leaving enough room for them to move. She looked up, noting the solid ice ceiling. The sky above them was deep blue, and she could also make out the lighter colour of some sort of structure in the distance around them, but the cage warped too much to make out details. The boar came into sharp focus, though, as it charged towards them again.

'Is this part of a Trial?' asked Abderos, and Evadne turned back towards him. Theseus groaned and she kneeled beside him on the floor.

'I'm surprised they put a captain in here if it is. But if there's one of us from each crew, I guess so. Theseus?' She poked him in the ribs and he tensed under his pale blue shirt, then sat bolt upright.

'Where am I?' he gasped as he looked around, before his gaze settled on Evadne.

'I don't know,' she answered, trying hard to ignore how beautiful his eyes were. 'We're in some sort of cage, made from ice. There's somebody from each crew here.' She gestured around her at the small holding cell. Theseus's eyes went wide as he looked over her shoulder. 'And there's a—' she was cut off by the clanging of the boar smashing into the cage wall behind her again. '... a giant boar trying to break in,' she finished.

'I see,' said Theseus slowly, pulling himself up onto his knees. He reached towards the ice and flinched when he touched it. 'Apollo,' he said.

'Apollo? The sun god? Really?' Abderos sounded incredulous.

'Who are you?' Theseus asked, turning to look at him.

'Abderos. Navigator on the *Alastor*.' There was no mistaking the pride in his voice, though Evadne thought he was young to be a navigator.

Theseus nodded at him. 'Apollo. Yes, I think so. Capricorn has the most extreme seasons in Olympus. There would be this much ice in winter. And it makes sense that Apollo's Trial would follow his twin sister's.'

'That doesn't explain why we're in here.'

'I assume we are the incentive to complete the Trial in a timely manner,' Evadne said, folding her arms across her chest. As if hearing her words, the boar's great tusks bounced off the ice cage again, the ringing sound rippling through the freezing air. Abderos's eyebrows knitted together.

'What do you mean?'

'She's right,' said Theseus, and Evadne suppressed her flash of joy at the praise. 'This cage won't withstand that battering for more than a couple of hours. So we'd better hope we either get rescued soon or our giant friend can wrestle boars.' They all looked down at the half-giant, still unconscious on the hard ground.

'We'll probably freeze before then anyway,' Evadne said, rubbing her bare arms as the ice rang around them.

3

ERYX

Eryx stared open-mouthed at the flame dish as the fire returned to its normal height, flickering orange again. Relief that it was Busiris in the cage instead of him caused him to sag slightly. He didn't know what he would have done if he'd had to spend another Trial watching from the sidelines. And although his chest was healing fast now, he doubted a stint in an ice cage would have helped it. He tried to feel bad about Busiris lying unconscious on the cage floor, but he couldn't. The gold-skinned man was a scheming coward and Eryx just couldn't muster up enough respect for him to feel sorry for him.

'Set a course for Capricorn,' said Antaeus gruffly. Albion grunted and turned towards the huge steering wheel. There was a loud thud behind them and Bergion yelled in surprise. A metallic ball rolled across the deck towards Antaeus and he stooped to pick it up.

Eryx leaned forward, his interest piqued. Detailed swirling patterns carved into the metal were glowing blue, and Eryx raised his eyebrows. It was the same as the sphere he had taken from the Hydra's head.

'A key...' he breathed. Antaeus looked at him.

'This is the same as the one you have?' Eryx nodded and Antaeus frowned.

'What do you think yours opens?' he asked. Eryx shrugged.

'I have no idea.' Bergion shoved past Eryx, peering at the ball.

'We need that to get Busiris back?' he said.

'Yeah. Looks like we're the blue team,' replied Antaeus. 'Go and get ready,' he told the giant. Bergion pulled at his beard and nodded, then heaved his way towards the hauler, his steps loud on the deck. Eryx looked up at his captain.

'You are taking me as well?' he said, painfully aware of the childlike, beseeching tone of his own voice.

'Brother...' Antaeus sighed. 'You are not fully healed. And you have no love for Busiris. You are not my first choice.' The words stung, though Eryx could hear the sense in them.

'I'm getting stronger by the minute, Captain. What if there are spaces or obstacles too small for a full giant? If we win one more task we'll be in the lead.'

'I'm well aware of that, Eryx. We're only as strong as our weakest link. And you are not my strongest option.'

Eryx scowled and made an effort not to stamp his foot. 'I can't just sit and watch a third Trial!' Anger made him shout and Antaeus straightened, the sympathy in his face fading.

'Fine. You two fight.' He pointed at Albion's back, as he stood at the wheel. 'The winner takes part.'

'Now?' Eryx said, slightly alarmed. Antaeus nodded.

'Now. Albion!' The fat giant spun around at hearing his name.

'One hour, Captain,' he said, assuming a progress report was wanted.

'Fight Eryx,' Antaeus ordered. 'The winner takes part in this Trial.'

Albion frowned. 'Why do I have to fight? Where's Bergion?' he said.

'Because I told you to. Get on with it!' Antaeus growled.

Albion bared his teeth briefly, then marched down the steps from the navigation wheel, to the middle of the huge Zephyr deck. Eryx followed him and poked as discreetly as he could at his own chest, testing for pain. He could feel none. He flexed his fists, hopping lightly from one foot to the other as he crossed the deck towards the giant. Albion had at least three feet on him, and likely ten stone, but he was much, much faster.

Albion smirked at him as he approached, rolling his massive shoulders and pulling up his black shorts. Eryx got on with the black-skinned brothers fine, and they all sparred regularly, but there was no way the giant was going to give him an easy ride just because he'd had an injury. Eryx crouched quickly, jumping back up, testing his thighs and warming his muscles. If he wanted to get down to Capricorn and take part in the Trial, he would have to prove himself.

'Begin!' roared Antaeus.

Eryx launched himself forward, ducking between Albion's legs as the giant swung for him. He twisted as he cleared the gap and sprang back up, coiling himself around the larger man's enormous shoulders. Albion spun around, trying to shake him off, and he tightened his legs around the fleshy waist and began beating the side of Albion's head with his fist.

'Yield!' he yelled.

Albion laughed, reaching up and grabbing for Eryx. He caught his shirt collar and pulled, dragging him over his shoulder and slamming him hard onto the deck in front of him. A tightness spread across Eryx's chest as he landed and he coughed. The pain lessened and he rolled to his feet, immediately ducking again as Albion stepped towards him with a well-aimed elbow. He threw his own elbow out as he darted past Albion, landing his blow in the back of the giant's knee and causing him to shout as he stumbled forward. He wheeled around and ran up Albion's flabby back, this time wrapping his arms around his neck and squeezing. Albion pulled at his arms, his huge, grimy fingers trying to dig between Eryx's arms and his own skin, but Eryx held on, trying to squeeze harder. Albion pushed himself back onto both feet, took a choking breath – and Eryx realised just in time what he was about to do. The giant began to fall backwards, and Eryx let go, landing awkwardly and scrabbling out of the way just before Albion's considerable weight crashed into the deck. The sound of wood splintering accompanied the giant's grunt.

'Enough!' roared Antaeus. 'I said fight, not destroy my ship!' His face was red as he stomped across the deck towards them. 'Albion, get this fixed, now!' Eryx leaned forward, offering his hand to Albion and trying not to laugh as the giant rolled around in the dent he'd made in the deck. Albion took it and Eryx heaved, helping him struggle to his feet. Pain gripped his chest again but he caught himself before he grimaced.

'Eryx, you're clearly fit. And having a smaller crew member may be a benefit. Go and get ready.' Antaeus didn't look at him as he spoke, still glaring at the broken wooden planks of the deck, so he missed Eryx's beaming grin.

4

HERCULES

Hercules stared out over the broad expanse of snow-covered land as the *Hybris* glided low over the surface of Capricorn. They were heading towards a bright white beacon of light shooting up from the ground. He had seen four beams rising from the surface as they had approached, but this one matched the harsh white light glowing from the sphere he was tossing from hand to hand.

'We'll reach the beam in ten minutes, Captain,' the minotaur said from the navigation wheel. He didn't answer.

HERCULES WAS WELL PRACTISED at containing his often-simmering temper. In fact, sometimes anger, ambition and excitement blurred together for him, melding into a constant stream of energy pushing him forward, fuelling his achievements. Today, though, he knew he was angry. Evadne had a made a fool of him and cost him the Trial on Sagittarius. Worse still, Lyssa had won.

His hand clenched hard around the cold metal key.

Evadne had given up. She had yielded. He knew he would have made it through the metal spikes and been victorious, but she had submitted for both of them. Without even knowing if it would cost them their lives. Artemis had said those who were worthy would be rescued.

A tiny part of him whispered unnervingly: *Worthy in whose eyes? Many would leave you to die.* But he crushed the thought immediately, refocusing on his blue-haired gunner. She would pay the price for her actions; would have done already if she hadn't been stolen away by the bloody gods themselves. The memory of the fear on her face when they had appeared back on the deck of the *Hybris,* when he had lifted her by the neck and let her see the rage within him, sent a shiver of pent-up energy through him. Let her fear of him grow in that cage. Let the apprehension of her impending punishment war with her need to be rescued by him. A small smile tugged at his lips. He would do what he could to make sure she was desperate to see him, as long as it didn't cost him the win.

5

LYSSA

The *Alastor* slowed as they soared over the source of the purple beam of light and Lyssa's mouth fell open slightly as she leaned over the railings. The light was shooting from the tallest spire of a castle made from shining ice, glittering like crystal. The castle crested a tall sheer peak that had been flattened at the top to accommodate the structure's many buildings, all joined together with elaborate walkways and tunnels. Spires of varying heights protruded from every building but were most concentrated in the central structure.

'Where should we moor?' Epizon asked, beside her. She focused on the ship, willing the *Alastor* to slow and descend, circling the peak.

'I think that's a dock.' She pointed to an outbuilding some way from the castle, at the edge of the flat peak. Epizon nodded.

'I'll check Phyleus is ready,' he said.

LYSSA EASED the ship to a stop by the dock, as tight to the

mountain as she could. As they got close, she realised that
the mountain itself was made from ice, not polished and
shiny like the buildings on top, but rough and coarse-look-
ing. She wondered what happened to the mountain, and the
castle, in summer. Maybe it didn't exist at all. She'd been to
Capricorn once before, but to the south of the island, and in
spring. It was nothing like this. The sparkling sky above
them was darker than usual, deep blue in colour, with
sheets of sparkling grey corkscrewing across her vision. A
cold wind whistled gently through the solar sails of the
Alastor and she let go of the railing to pull her heavy leather
cloak tighter around herself.

'Bet you're glad you kept me on board now,' Phyleus
said. She turned to him, eyebrows raised in question. 'You
know who paid for that cloak?' he said, nodding at it. She
scowled and turned away. He was right, though. They'd had
no cold-weather provisions, and no hope of getting any,
until he had bought his way onto the ship. She sniffed
loudly, then heard clopping on the wooden deck.

'Good luck, Captain. I wish I could help,' Nestor said as
she approached.

'Thank you. You'll be with us on the next one, I promise.'

'I hope so.' Len trotted up next to her, ducking and
pulling a face as her tail flicked next to him.

'Bring him back quickly, Cap,' he said. Lyssa gave him a
tight smile.

'We will. Are we ready?'

'Yes, Captain,' Epizon's voice rang out over Phyleus's.

'Good. Let's go get Abderos,' she said, and vaulted over
the railing onto the pier below. Her left boot slipped as she
landed, her heart leaping into her mouth and her arms
shooting out on instinct, flailing for purchase. Strong hands
gripped her from behind as her foot came back down on

the icy surface. 'Thanks,' she gasped, taking a gulping breath.

'No problem,' Phyleus muttered. She whirled around, almost falling again at the sound of his voice. She had thought it was Epizon who had caught her.

Phyleus grinned broadly as he saw her surprise. She glared at him a moment, then faced the castle, hoping her pink cheeks could be blamed on the cold.

'Do we go to the tallest spire? To where the light is?' Epizon asked.

'I guess so,' she said and began to walk, carefully, towards the castle.

THEY HAD BARELY REACHED the towering archway at the base of the castle walls when a flicker of purple caught Lyssa's eye. She paused, looking for the streak of light that had crossed her peripheral vision.

'What...' started Phyleus, then he spun around on the spot.

'Did you see it?' she asked.

'Purple light,' he said, staring intently around the empty castle grounds.

'There!' said Epizon. A slither of purple light was hovering to their right, away from the castle building. She stepped towards it and it blurred, reappearing a few feet further away.

'Are we supposed to follow it?' Phyleus sounded wary.

'We followed the light all the way to Capricorn. No point not trusting it now,' she said, and stepped deliberately after it.

'You were saying?' Phyleus commented a few minutes later, as they watched the light reach the brink of the peak, then disappear over the edge. When none of them moved any closer, the light reappeared and performed the same stunt, flickering in the eerily quiet twilight.

'If Apollo wants us to go over, then we go over,' Lyssa said, squaring her shoulders and pulling down the hood that covered her red curls.

'What? Are you crazy?' Phyleus stomped to the edge of the mountain, then leaned out carefully. 'It's pretty much a sheer drop,' he said, shaking his head. The purple light shimmered into existence beside him, then dived off the edge. Lyssa looked at Epizon and raised her eyebrows in silent question.

'If that's what we've got to do, then that's what we do,' he said calmly, then pulled the pack off his shoulder and started rummaging. He waved Phyleus over to him. 'Here,' he said, and handed him two metal handles the size of a fist, covered in curved hooks. 'Claws. They'll help grip the ice.'

Phyleus took them mutely, looking between Lyssa and her huge first mate. 'You're serious?' he checked as she got her own claws out of her deep cloak pockets and stepped up to the edge of the mountain. She didn't look down, instead turning her back to the precipice and dropping to her knees. 'I don't know why I'm surprised,' Phyleus muttered, his voice carrying on the cold breeze.

'Phyleus, you know what I'm going to say,' she called. 'If you don't like it...' She paused as she pushed the claw in her right hand into the ice and tugged at it experimentally. It held.

'Go back to the ship,' Phyleus answered in a high-pitched imitation of her voice.

'Exactly.' She took a deep breath and eased herself backwards off the precipice. She gasped at the moment of weightlessness as her feet found no purchase on the surface below her. But her strong arms held fast on the claws and the ice was rough enough for her boots to grip eventually and take some of her weight. Adrenaline hummed through her body and she tuned out everything around her, focusing on nothing but removing one claw at a time from the ice and making steady progress down the vertical mountain. Every now and then she called out one of the others' names, relief buoying her when she heard Epizon's measured response or Phyleus's strained one. Epizon was strong enough to climb using just his arms and the claws, so she had little worry for him, but though Phyleus was fit, his strength was no match for either of them. On some level she knew it was unfair that he had been through every Trial so far, but she couldn't help feeling like he deserved it. He hadn't earned his place on the *Alastor*, so he could damn well risk his life for it now.

Her anger made her jab the claw in her left hand too hard into the ice and a splintering crack formed, creeping across the craggy surface. She drew a breath, reminding herself she needed to concentrate, and pushed Phyleus out of her head.

6

HEDONE

'Psyche, I don't think I can do it,' Hedone murmured, staring at the streak of red light that was launching itself off the edge of the mountain for the twentieth time.

'Of course you can. Bellerephon is already most of the way down!' Psyche's exasperated tone cut through Hedone's apprehension. Her desire to hold her team up and give Hercules his best chance of winning was warring with her increasing desire to impress the fierce woman before her. 'If you can't do it, then you need to go back. If that boar gets to Theseus...' Fire flashed in Psyche's eyes and guilt forced Hedone forward, nearer to the brink.

'It's just...' She peered over the edge, very real fear skittering through her. 'It's just such a long way down. And I don't know if I'm strong enough.'

'You *are* strong enough. And you have ice claws on your hands and your feet.' Psyche gestured to her boots, covered with metal studs that bit into the snow. 'Just follow me, and you'll be fine.' Psyche held her gaze until she nodded.

'Crouch, backwards,' she said and demonstrated. Hedone copied her, turning her back nervously to the precipice and dropping quickly to her knees. 'Good. Now dig in the claws and don't look down.' Hedone glanced sideways at Psyche, watched her push the metal spiked gloves into the ice and did the same. The leather was thick enough to keep out the cold, and when she wiggled her hand the gloves didn't move. Taking a long breath she shuffled backwards, gasping as she felt her feet move out over nothingness.

'That's good. As soon as your knees are over, kick your toes into the ice,' called Psyche.

'Right,' she mumbled back, her mouth dry. She did as she was told, only moving her hands a few inches at a time as she lowered herself over the edge.

'There you go,' said Psyche. Hedone looked to her left, where Psyche was perched only a few feet away, her claws deep in the ice. 'Now, just move down. Concentrate, and before you know it, you'll be on the ground.'

'Uh-huh,' she replied, facing the mountain and closing her eyes a moment. She was vertical, the claws holding her against a sheet of ice a hundred feet above the ground. She felt sick. *What was she doing*? She dragged the image of Hercules's face to the forefront of her mind, picturing the lines of his smile, the promise in his eyes. She was doing this for him. She was proving herself to him. She couldn't sit around on the *Virtus*, unable to help or hinder.

She pulled her right hand away from the ice, the claw coming loose, her body wobbling and her breath catching. Panic threatened to overcome her but her arm moved instinctively, shoving hard into the ice again lower down. Instantly she felt sturdier and the vibration in her legs lessened. She pulled her left hand out, not wanting to give the panic a chance to take hold. As soon as she had it firmly back in the ice, she moved her right leg. One by one, she moved her limbs: right hand, left hand, right foot, left foot. Years stuck meditating in a temple had left her good at counting and breathing, emptying her mind of anything else. Even the cold faded from her awareness as she moved down the face of the mountain.

She was so surprised when her foot hit the ground that she cried out.

'Are you all right?' Bellerephon was there, reaching for her as she dared to look over her shoulder. After focusing on the bright ice for so long, her eyes streamed as she looked around. She had made it. Relief washed over her as her second foot connected with the solid earth through crunching snow. There was a soft thud as Psyche jumped the last few inches and landed beside her. She was beaming. It was the first proper smile Hedone thought she had ever given her.

'Well done,' she said and Hedone couldn't help smiling back. She'd done it. And got there before Psyche! 'Keep the claws on your boots, there's likely to be more ice terrain,' she said, and scanned their surroundings.

Hedone followed her gaze. She realised, belatedly, that snow was falling softly, catching in her dark hair, and she pulled up the deep hood of her fur cloak. The uneven ground was already covered in the white powder and though less light filtered down to them, it glistened off the reflective surface. Curving bare rocks jutted out of the ground regularly, looking like giant teeth. It was hard to make out what was in the distance as the snow seemed to swirl more thickly, but it looked fairly flat. The streak of red light was hovering ahead of them, zipping off a few feet, then returning, clearly wanting them to follow.

'Let's go,' said Psyche, pulling up her hood.

LYSSA

I t was colder down on the frozen earth. Lyssa huddled inside her cloak, trying to disappear further into it as they crossed the snowy expanse. The wind was still gentle save for the small flurries that crossed their path periodically, smattering them in cold powder. It was quiet, the only sound the crunching of their boots on the snow, and they had seen nothing living as they followed the purple light. To either side of them and ahead there was just more white. Lyssa had seen snow before, atop mountains on Leo, but never in this quantity and never seemingly endless.

'Do you think the others have an identical route to the middle?' asked Phyleus. Lyssa thought about it. It would be fairest if so. Which meant nothing. The gods were far from fair. She shoved away the image of her mother that began to flicker in her mind.

'Maybe. Who knows?'

'I think it's likely. Hercules only has one other crew member. Hopefully that will hinder him,' Epizon said, his voice carrying on the wind.

'Would that mean Evadne dies?' asked Phyleus quietly. Lyssa looked sideways at him, raising an eyebrow.

'I don't know,' she said. 'Twelve *deadly* Trials.'

'Not a nice way to go, being eaten by a giant boar,' he said eventually.

'Huh,' Lyssa grunted. Evadne had made a choice when she joined that maniac on the *Hybris*. She would have known the risks, known who Hercules was. If anyone from that ship got torn apart by a wild boar Lyssa would struggle to feel sorrow.

'THERE'S A LAKE AHEAD,' said Epizon, slowing slightly.

'More ice,' groaned Phyleus. Ten feet ahead of them the uneven snowy ground they'd been walking on gave way to a glittering frozen lake, seeming to create more light. It stretched on and on, its far bank barely visible in the distance.

'Do you think we can walk on it?' asked Lyssa, casting a nervous glance at Epizon. He weighed at least twice what she and Phyleus did.

'We'd better hope so. I can't see a way around.' Epizon was looking from right to left but the polished lake surface shone as far as they could see. The purple light bounced ahead of them, over the lake, and paused, waiting for them to catch up.

PHYLEUS PUT his foot out first, testing the ice. It was crystal clear and sparkled like glass. He pushed his toe against it, then eased the rest of his foot down. He looked at them both.

'Feels good,' he said. Epizon reached out, gripping

Phyleus's shoulder, ready to pull him back, as he lifted his other leg off the ground and put his whole weight on the frozen surface. When nothing happened, Phyleus grinned. 'Let's go,' he said and turned to start walking.

A dark shadow swept across the lake and he froze. 'What was that?'

'I don't know.' Lyssa narrowed her eyes as she fervently scanned the twilight sky for the source of the shadow.

'Why are you looking up there?' Phyleus said, an edge to his voice. 'It was under the ice!'

Lyssa snapped her eyes to the lake. Phyleus nodded.

'It was quite big,' Epizon said.

Lyssa's skin began to tingle, her power thrumming through her in anticipation. 'Then let's not break the ice,' she said and stepped out after Phyleus.

SHE HELD her breath as Epizon stepped carefully onto the ice. It didn't move, looking as solid as earth as he hesitantly shuffled towards her.

'Shuffling doesn't suit you,' she told him, and started towards the opposite bank. The ice was so clear she could see right down into the murky blue depths below. Nothing stirred, and she could see no rocks or plants, or a bottom to the lake. They all took slow, careful steps and she quickly found that walking with her feet sticking out to either side felt more stable on the smooth surface. She hoped Phyleus didn't spot her doing it, though, as waddling probably didn't look very captain-like.

The shadow passed under them again when they were twenty feet across. It was big, but not bigger than Epizon, and it moved too fast for any of them to get a look at what it was, only to see that it was very bright blue. Exchanging looks but saying nothing the three of them continued onwards, following the impatient streak purple of light that was zipping about in front of them.

'I think we're halfway,' Epizon said. Lyssa looked up from the depths below her feet and glanced behind her at the bank they'd left, at the mountain crested by the castle a long way off in the distance.

A loud crack ripped her attention back to the ice and she saw the shadow shoot beneath her, a massive crack in the ice following its path.

'The ice is splitting!' called Phyleus, a few feet in front of her. She looked up, seeing cracks forming everywhere, snaking towards each other as the blue thing in the water below zigzagged across the lake at lightning speed.

'Run!' she shouted, and let her Rage flood through her, feeling strength fill her arms and legs as she began sprinting towards the bank. She overtook Phyleus quickly, cursing him for not moving faster as the cracking sounds around them became deafening. Epizon yelled and she skidded to a halt, her left leg sliding out from underneath her. She spun around as she fell, managing to keep her other foot flat on the ice. Epizon was on both knees, covering his head as a streak of brightest blue burst from the lake, water and lumps of ice showering down over him. Lyssa scrabbled back to her feet, launching herself towards her first mate.

'Wait!' Phyleus was shouting behind her but she ignored him, willing Epizon to get back to his feet as she leaped over a widening crack. She landed well and was only a few feet from Epizon, who was still covering his head, when there was a shrieking squawk. She threw herself flat against the ice as the blue creature swooped over her, spraying her with freezing water. She rolled onto her back and gaped.

The thing was a bird now, beating its massive wings in

place above her. Its plumage ranged through every shade of blue she could imagine and its beak and eyes were solid white. Rippling pale blue feathers crested its head, dancing like flames. Every beat of its wings sent a paralysing gust of air over her, so cold she felt even her bones were freezing. Then it squawked again, gave a mighty flap and soared away, high into the sky. Convulsive shivering overtook Lyssa's body and she tried to roll back onto her front, to push herself back to her feet.

'Eppppiiizzzoonnn,' she said through madly chattering teeth as she slowly got up.

He moved his shaking arms away from his head. His normally deep-brown lips white with cold.

'I'mmmm allll righhhttt,' he chattered back, shaking his chest and arms. He rubbed at his face as she staggered towards him, trying to shake the cold out of her own limbs.

'Lyssa!' She turned around on hearing Phyleus's voice and her stomach dropped. The solid surface of the lake was now in pieces, lumps of ice slowly knocking into each other as they floated on the water. She and Epizon were on one large piece, barely moving on the water, but Phyleus was crouching on his hands and knees on a much smaller piece some distance away.

'That was an ice phoenix,' he called over to them. She looked at Epizon and he shrugged and slapped at his own cheek, some of his colour returning.

'Why didn't it kill us?' She'd ask him later how he knew what it was.

Phyleus stood up as carefully as he could on his small island of ice.

'It may have. I think the ice is melting.'

8

ERYX

Eryx had never been so cold in his life. It was like the bird was sucking more than just the heat from his body. It was suffusing him with a cold so deep, so debilitating that it paralysed him, rendering him unable to even think about anything but the sensation of freezing. And then, as suddenly as the bird had burst from the lake, it was gone, soaring into the sky. Eryx quivered, his skin stinging as he tried to flex his fists, move his head.

'Eryx!' His captain roared.

'Cccaapppptaaiiinn,' he stuttered back as loudly as he could, blinking and rolling his neck. Bergion was on his back beside him on the frozen lake. 'Bbbeerrrgggiooon?'

The giant grunted and pulled himself up to a sitting position. As he did so the ice beneath them moved and Eryx stumbled on his shivering legs. It was cracking, he realised slowly.

'Don't move,' shouted Antaeus. Eryx rotated on the spot carefully, looking around him properly. The surface of the lake was in pieces, islands of ice floating everywhere. Some were still huge, like the piece they were on, but others wouldn't take his weight, let alone that of the two full giants. Antaeus was further behind them. It had taken his captain an age to get this far, his vast bodyweight making him nervous enough to move painfully slowly across the ice. How was he going to get across now?

'Ccccan we mmmove the bbit of ice we're on?' Bergion said. Eryx looked down, through the crystal-clear ice to the depths of the lake.

'No,' he answered, relieved his own teeth had stopped chattering. 'Even if we had poles, which we don't, the lake's too deep.' He turned around, looking at Antaeus. There were three or four islands of ice between them, the gaps growing and closing as they ebbed on the water. 'Can you jump?' he called. Antaeus shook his head.

'I'm too heavy. They'll sink when I land.' Antaeus kneeled and reached his arm over the edge of the shard of ice. He raised his eyebrows as he dipped his hand into the lake, before whipping it out again immediately.

'Gods, that's cold,' he swore. Slowly, he did it again, pushing his hand in a long stroke though the water. The ice island floated forward, bumping gently against another bit of ice.

Eryx looked at his own island. It was too big to paddle, even with two of them. 'Bergion, we need to split up, get on smaller islands and then paddle.'

The giant nodded and eased himself to his feet. The ice rocked beneath them. With a deep breath Eryx backed up a few careful steps, then ran, giving himself little time to think about what would happen if he missed his landing spot. As he reached the edge of the ice he jumped. He realised as he was in the air that he had jumped too far. He was going to overshoot the island he had aimed for. He kicked his legs as he came down, trying to turn and slow his momentum. He landed badly on one knee and skidded, throwing his hands out and scratching uselessly at the polished ice to try to slow himself down. Fear clawed its way up his throat as his straight leg went off the side of the island and blistering cold wrapped around his foot. He scrabbled, using the knee he still had on the ice to push himself forward, flat onto his front. The ice tipped beneath him and mercifully levelled, halting his slide. He panted as he pulled himself to his feet, adrenaline coursing through his body. Bergion was gaping at him from the other island, frost smattering his dark beard.

'I'm not doing that,' he said and folded his arms.

'Get on with it!' roared Antaeus, who was heaving ice islands out of his way, using them to pull his own along in the water. 'These are melting!'

In alarm, Eryx looked down, then around. It was true. More water was visible, and less ice – the islands were shrinking. Bergion took a few steps back, then ran, leaping for an island half the size of the one he was currently on. He landed with a thud right in the middle, managing not to slide. His glee was cut short however as a loud crack sounded.

'Move!' yelled Eryx as a crack spread out from under the giant's feet. Bergion leaped to one side, the ice rocking as the island split completely in two.

'You're too heavy. Paddle!' called Antaeus. Bergion dropped to his knees, yelping as he put his gloved hand into the freezing water, then splashing as he tried to propel himself forward. Eryx looked down at his own feet, one boot sodden wet and freezing, then up at the distant bank they were aiming for, where the streak of blue light they were following danced at the lake's edge.

He knew the fastest way to get to the other side. Backing

up, he moved as lightly as he could, up on his toes, exactly as he had been taught to as a boxer. Then he ran and jumped. As soon as his feet touched the ice of the next island he launched himself forward, not allowing time for his boots to slide on the ice. A few bounds across the island and he was jumping again, twisting slightly in the air towards the next gently floating platform. He kept going, flying across the ice, leaping and landing with feet lighter than they should be. He knew he couldn't stop or miss – his momentum would take him all the way to the bottom of that freezing lake. And then he landed on crunching snow, his movements slowing without the shining ice to propel him on, but his strong legs still urging him forward. He slowed as the blue light whizzed around him, bending over and taking long breaths as he came to a stop. He'd made it.

He turned and looked back at the lake. Antaeus was close now, grabbing the edges of the larger bits of ice and pulling his diminishing vessel along. Bergion was far behind, splashing as he tried to move his larger ice island. Eryx walked slowly back to the bank.

'Come on, Bergion, you're almost there!' he shouted, projecting as much encouragement as he could into his voice. A few feet to his right Antaeus's island bumped against the bank. Eryx jogged over, bending to hold the ice steady as his captain crawled across it before sighing loudly as he transferred his weight to the hard, snow-covered ground. Eryx let go of the island and turned to his captain, then drew a sharp breath. Antaeus was sitting back on his heels, holding up his hands. The fingertips were white, and the pale colour was creeping down towards his palms.

'Frostbite,' said Antaeus, dully. 'I need to get them warm.' He paused. 'Though it may already be too late.'

9

EVADNE

'For the last time, there's nothing we can do about being in here!' Evadne was losing patience. The gold-skinned giant had done nothing but panic and whine since he had woken up. As he scowled at her, she silently thanked Zeus she didn't have to share a ship with this coward.

'It's all right for you, you're small. This cage must feel like a palace,' he hissed.

She raised her eyebrows. 'We're *all* trapped in here!'

'Yes, trapped *together*. So we may as well try to get on with each other, until we're rescued,' said Theseus calmly. He was sitting on the floor next Abderos's wheelchair, his knees up, looking for all the world like nothing was wrong. Evadne huffed and continued her pacing.

'You're not helping, with all the pacing,' said Busiris, jumping as the clang of the boar's impact rang through the cage. Evadne had all but stopped noticing it now.

'Fine,' she snapped and sat down hard on the floor, crossing her legs. There was a long, awkward silence.

'So. Who do you reckon will get here first?' said

Abderos. Nobody answered. Evadne wanted to say Hercules, wanted to immediately back her captain, but she couldn't. Hercules had only two people now, and one of them had hooves. Not ideal for icy and snowy terrain. Busiris scowled again.

'Antaeus, obviously. Giants don't feel the cold like humans.'

'Is that right?' said Evadne, looking at him. 'In that case you don't need that shirt.' Busiris barked a laugh. 'You want my shirt? Not a chance.'

Evadne shook her head. 'Thought as much.'

'Do you want mine?' offered Theseus. For a fraction of a second she was tempted to say yes, if only to be able to look at Theseus shirtless for a time. But Hercules's fury when she'd last seen him flashed into her mind. What would he say when he got here and she was wearing the shirt of his rival? She shook her head again, but without the angry expression.

'No, I'm fine. Thank you.'

'What do you do on your ship?' asked Abderos.

'Stop trying to make conversation. We're not friends. Any of us,' she said.

'We don't need to be enemies,' said Theseus. She ignored him and began picking angrily at her fingernails. It was easy to be rude to the boy in the chair or the cowardly giant, but being rude to Theseus didn't feel right.

'Is it true the *Virtus* has a pool below decks?' Abderos spoke again, this time to Theseus, who laughed; and the sound was nice. Evadne looked up from scowling at her hands, despite herself.

'No. No, that's not true. Where did you hear that?'

Abderos shrugged. 'Around. How fast does she go?'

'You're the navigator on the *Alastor,* right? She's one hell of a fast ship,' Theseus replied, looking up at Abderos's eager face.

The boy nodded proudly. 'That she is. She's old, sure, but Crosswinds are all fast, and Captain Lyssa, well, she has...' He trailed off, suspicion suddenly taking over his expression. Evadne laughed, sneering.

'We know Lyssa channels her power into her ship. It's not a secret. She makes it pretty obvious.'

'Well, how come your captain doesn't, then?' he retorted. She looked away. She'd wondered the same thing since Lyssa had showed how fast she could go on Sagittarius.

'You have to have an extremely strong bond with a ship, to be able to share your power with it. With anything, in fact,' said Theseus. He gestured at Evadne. 'Your captain does the same thing with that sword, *Keravnos*. The wielder needs to share the same goals as the object, so completely that it becomes a part of them. Lyssa's goal is to fly. Fast. I don't know what drives that need for her, but that's all the ship wants too. For Hercules and the sword...' He shrugged. 'The need is to destroy.'

Evadne swallowed and looked back down at her hands. To destroy. No wonder his daughter needed to fly, to escape. The thought had settled in her mind before she could expel it, and she was instantly angry with herself. She was on Hercules's crew. She knew what he had done to his wife and child, what Hera had made him do.

Doubt gnawed at her. What he *said* Hera made him do. She had seen that temper now. She had glimpsed what he was capable of. She took a deep breath and subconsciously touched her neck where he had gripped her, lifted her off her feet, ready to punish her for saving their lives.

He had a lot at stake, she told herself. Of course his temper would be frayed. The Trials had not gone as he had hoped so far, the world was watching and the pressure was huge. She thought about when he was happy, his smile and his charisma and his awesome aura of power. He would win and they would live together in immortality. She was sure of it. She just needed to deal with the bumps and bruises along the way.

10

HERCULES

Hercules stamped across the snow, cursing his first mate. Asterion had done nothing but slow him down when they'd crossed the lake. He could hear the minotaur grunting behind him as he struggled to keep up.

'Captain, I need to do something about my leg,' he said, his gruff voice strained. Hercules closed his eyes as he stopped. He needed to win this Trial. He wasn't willing to go against Zeus and try again on his own, he reasoned, so he needed to do what he could to get Asterion moving faster. He turned. The minotaur was still wet to his chest from where he had slid into the water. His dark fur was matted to his skin under his leather armour and Hercules could see he was shaking. The leg he had referred to was paler than the rest of his body at the ankle, a white tinge spreading to his angular knee.

'Looks like frostbite,' Hercules said. 'Give me the pack. We can rest a short while.' Asterion sagged with relief as he shrugged out of the leather pack slung over his shoulder and handed it over.

. . .

HERCULES DUG the snow off a patch of the barren ground and had a small fire going within minutes. It was getting colder, he thought. Taking a break to gather a bit of warmth was probably what everyone else was doing. They shouldn't lose any time here. He scanned his surroundings. Behind him the lake was now completely clear of ice. To his left and right an expanse of white was all he could see for miles, swirling snow moving past the occasional stark tree or rock. Ahead of him, though, behind the dancing white light, was a mountain shaped like a claw. It rose majestically, curving gently to a sharp point. If there was more climbing to do he would have to help Asterion. The bull-man had strong arms but hooves and ice were a hopeless mix.

Hercules found himself wishing that Asterion had been taken, and Evadne was with him. She was tough, for a girl, and would probably have fared better than his first mate so far. Maybe he should just leave him behind. He turned back to the fire. Asterion was holding his hooved foot out beside it, rubbing and punching the skin. Water frozen into his fur was melting and dripping onto the ground, sinking quickly through the powdery snow.

Asterion looked up at him. 'It is helping, I think.' Hercules nodded. 'Thank you,' the minotaur said, quietly.

Hercules looked away, back at the mountain. 'Ten minutes. Then we leave.'

'Yes, Captain.'

11

LYSSA

Lyssa watched as Phyleus held his hands over the tiny fire, wincing and poking at his little finger. A weird white colour was creeping down from his fingernail.

'Do you think it'll fall off?' said Epizon.

Phyleus looked at him in alarm. 'I bloody hope not!' he said, rubbing at it.

Lyssa rolled her eyes. 'It'll be fine, just get it warm. Besides, it's only a finger.'

Phyleus raised his eyebrows at her.

'Only a finger?' he repeated slowly. 'Only a finger? I need my fingers!'

'Just be pleased we got across the lake at all,' she snapped, looking sideways at Epizon. Her first mate nearly hadn't, the ice tipping and rocking under his weight so much that at times she had been convinced she'd lose him to the freezing depths. Phyleus glared at her and she held his angry look. 'How do you know what that bird was?' she asked.

'Saw one once.' Lyssa cocked her head at him. 'In a

book,' he said quickly. 'I haven't actually seen a real one before. I don't think they're much into eating or killing people, phoenixes.' He flexed his little finger as he spoke. 'Just messing with lakes, apparently. It was beautiful, though, wasn't it?'

Lyssa frowned. 'Beautiful? Did you feel the cold? Like you would never, ever be warm again?'

Phyleus looked at her and shook his head. 'No, I was too far away.'

'You wouldn't be calling it beautiful if you had. It was horrible.'

THEY LAPSED INTO SILENCE, taking it in turns to warm their hands and dry their boots over the small fire. Lyssa looked at the claw-shaped mountain ahead of them, looming large but distant. It was not going to be fun trekking across the snow to reach it. But the purple light streaked about them, encouraging them to follow. Epizon pulled the pack back onto his shoulder and stood up, stamping on the fire.

'Ready?'

'Let's go,' she answered, not waiting for Phyleus to reply.

IT WAS EVEN HARDER than she had thought it would be. The closer to the mountain they got, the more the wind picked up, until a howling snowstorm was whirling around them. All they could see through the stinging flakes was the purple light, dancing back every time they lost sight of it. Lyssa pulled the hood of her cloak as low over her face as she could without completely restricting her vision. The snow was so deep around her boots now that each step was becoming harder, as she needed to lift her legs higher and higher. She looked sideways at Phyleus. To his credit, he was only just starting to fall behind her. She was acutely aware of her power, the strength humming through her body, willing her forward, and she wasn't sure how she would have coped without it. Climbing down the sheer peak and then racing across the frozen lake would tire anybody out.

She slowed, stepping awkwardly sideways in the snow to fall in beside Phyleus. He looked across at her from inside his hood, surprised.

'Didn't think you liked talking to me,' he said, loudly so she could hear him over the wind.

'Just wanted to point out that you're holding us up,' she said. He gave her a sarcastic smile as he kicked through piled-high snow. 'Lift your leg over it, instead of through it. You won't get so cold,' she said.

'You been around snow before?' he said, lifting his leg higher on his next step.

'Yeah. Lots of snow on the mountain in Leo. I used to like walking, spending time as high up as I could get.'

'Close to the skies,' Phyleus said. She looked at him, surprised.

'I guess so. Though I never thought about it like that at the time.' She hadn't. She'd just loved being higher than the rest of the world. She hadn't known she wanted to fly on a ship until she'd run away from her father.

'You know, we really should talk about the end of the race on Sagittarius,' Phyleus said. She scowled.

'Why?'

'The sails. They were turning black. I think that's important.' He slowed, fully turning towards her as he spoke. 'Lyssa, has that ever happened before?'

'It's *Captain*, not Lyssa!' Anger laced her voice and she

knew it was nothing to do with what he had called her. His face hardened.

'*Captain*, we need to talk about your Rage,' he said slowly.

'You don't know me, or my ship! Why the hell would I talk to you about my power?' She stamped through the snow, not noticing herself speed up.

'Because I was there, I saw the sails, I saw you. Do you know you were smiling? Smiling like a maniac as we hurtled towards those spikes. That's not normal!'

'Don't you dare tell me what's normal!' She whirled on him, not caring as her hood flew back, the roar of the wind loud. 'Do you think anything about my life is normal? Anything about my past, the *Alastor*, my future? You come from your rich family, loafing around Olympus doing whatever you please, whenever you please, and you think you can tell me how to live my life?' She was shocked to find tears pricking the corners of her eyes. Her Rage simmered, but didn't push her. This wasn't anger, this was sorrow, she realised. Phyleus stared at her, mouth tightly shut. 'You will never, ever understand me,' she snarled and pulled her hood back up, storming towards the mountain, leaving Phyleus standing in the snow.

Whoever came across the Python would die, until Apollo, an expert archer, shot her with a perfect arrow. She fell to the floor, taking huge gasps of air and thrashing around. She writhed on the ground hissing, her life eventually leaving her.

EXCERPT FROM

HYMN TO APOLLO BY HOMER

Written 600–500 B.C.

Paraphrased by Eliza Raine

12

HEDONE

Hedone would be happy if she never saw snow again. The wind seemed to pick up handfuls of it, endlessly hurling it at their frozen bodies as they trudged closer to the ugly mountain. Whatever they found there couldn't be worse than the threat of sinking to the bottom of an ice-cold lake, she thought. One of her few physical strengths was running, and she weighed so little it had been relatively easy to get across the melting lake quickly. But Bellerephon had slipped and the fear she had felt for him as Psyche raced to pull him out had been very real. She shuddered. As much as she wanted to help Hercules, she was starting to think that this was not the Trial to do so. She didn't know anything about his progress and concentrating on keeping herself and Theseus alive seemed the best use of her time.

As they got close to the mountain the wind died down, as shelter was provided by the enormous rock structure. The bouncing red light led them closer and closer, until it loomed over them, the curved peak now completely blocking the snow. Psyche pushed back her hood and looked up, shaking snow from her cloak. Hedone followed suit.

The light suddenly zipped off, heading straight for the mountain. As it arrived there was a glow, slight at first, then stronger and stronger, spreading into a large rectangle. A door, Hedone realised. Relief that they would be inside, out of the relentless weather was quickly replaced by apprehension. Nothing had been easy so far, and it was unlikely to become so now.

When they got close the red light faded, revealing a dark tunnel in the rock face, sloping gently downwards. Hedone glanced at Psyche, who motioned for them to stop. Bellerephon pulled the pack from his shoulder and dug around in it, whilst Psyche took a knife from her own. When Bellepheron had armed himself with his slingshot they descended, hesitantly, into the mountain.

THE CAVE they entered was stunning. High, vaulted ceilings had been carved from the stone, and ice pillars, made by stalagmites and stalactites meeting one another, joined the floor to the ceiling at random intervals. Dancing under the ice was a shimmering blue light, similar to the ice phoenix's crest. It looked like liquid fire, warping and rippling behind the glassy surface.

It was mesmerising. Hedone stepped towards a pillar, her hand outstretched, but Psyche batted her arm down.

'No. Don't touch anything,' she muttered. Hedone frowned but obeyed. They walked slowly through the cave, her eyes wide with wonder at the ethereal patterns the blue flames made under the ice. The cavern seemed to go on forever in every direction, but the light from each pillar only extended a few feet, making it hard to tell. Their red light bobbed along ahead of them, guiding them in the direction it wanted them to go, and they followed, silently.

Silently enough that she heard the hiss behind them. She froze at the same time as the others.

'What was that?' she whispered, afraid to turn around. Psyche and Bellerephon had already spun around to face the other way, slingshot and knife raised. Hedone watched as Bellerephon's eyes widened, fear rolling though her.

'Run!' yelled Psyche and turned, sprinting after the red light. Hedone raced after her, focusing on her glinting golden armour exposed by her flapping cloak. Bellerephon raced past on her other side, legs pumping. There was an earthy slithering sound, like something massive being dragged along the ground.

'What is it?' panted Hedone, not slowing.

'Python,' gasped Psyche between breaths, as a golden snake as thick as a giant's arm slithered across their path.

13

LYSSA

'Captain, I don't like the look of this.'

Lyssa looked around at the glittering cavern. Epizon was right. It was too pretty, too peaceful to be trusted.

'These are incredible,' said Phyleus, reaching out and touching the ice column where the blue flames danced and swirled inside. The second he touched it, the blue dimmed. Not just on the column he touched, but everywhere, the whole cave plunging into flickering semi-darkness.

'Shit,' he said, pulling his hand back.

'Idiot,' Lyssa hissed. A moving flash of gold caught her eye, standing out against the purple glow of the guiding light. 'There's something in here,' she said, her muscles clenching as her power built in anticipation. There it was again, higher this time. She looked up at the column where she'd seen it, her breath catching. A golden snake was coiled around the pillar, the dim blue lights reflecting off its lithe body.

'Doesn't Apollo have something to do with pythons?' whispered Epizon.

'Looks like it, yeah,' she muttered back. 'What do we do?' As if in answer the purple light tore off, zipping between the pillars away from them.

'Follow it!' she shouted, and ran.

SHE'D BARELY GOT ten feet before Phyleus screamed. She turned and snarled as she saw Phyleus, immobile as the gold body of the snake coiled slowly around his thighs. The snake was long, she realised. Part of it was still wrapped around the pillar, where she had first noticed it. Phyleus whimpered as the snake's head rose around his front, a forked white tongue flicking out with a hiss.

'Help me,' he said through gritted teeth, his eyes finding hers. She leaped at the snake with a roar, clearing the distance instantly. Rage flooded through her muscles, her skin feeling aflame as she grabbed the snake behind its head and squeezed. It thrashed and she stamped as hard as she could on its glimmering body. She felt the muscle give beneath her foot and the head thrashed harder but she knew she was stronger. She closed her fist hard and yanked, smashing the snake's head into the nearest ice pillar and pulling Phyleus, still wrapped in its coils, off his feet.

But even as she did so she regretted it. The pillar shattered completely as the snake went limp. Tiny blue flames rippled out into the cavern, bouncing and dancing as they dispersed and Lyssa raced to Phyleus, who was desperately trying to remove himself from the heavy coils. She pulled the lifeless body of the snake from him with ease as a deep rumbling began.

'Thanks, but I'm pretty sure we weren't supposed to destroy the cave,' said Phyleus, scrambling to his feet. She didn't answer but shoved him towards Epizon and the purple light. The rumbling was growing louder and the cave began to shudder under her feet as they ran, the purple light getting faster as the cavern got darker. She could hear rushing water. A sick, cold fear came over her. If this cavern filled with water... They would drown.

She powered after the light, not daring to look back for the source of the growing sound of rushing water. They weaved in and out of columns, the blue lights inside now muted and dull. Again Lyssa felt a grudging respect for Phyleus, racing along next to her, his stamina admirable for a mortal human. The purple light jumped abruptly and they all slowed, looking up as it reached the vaulted ceiling of the cave, then dived back down.

'Woah!' yelled Epizon, flinging his arms out and coming to a complete stop. Lyssa almost bowled into him, still watching the light fall and missing what was right in front of her. They were standing on a cliff's edge, the source of the sound a roaring waterfall across a gaping chasm. The water poured into the cavern below, and Lyssa gaped as the purple light plunged past them.

'I'm not going down there.' Phyleus folded his arms against his heaving chest.

'For once, I agree with you,' she panted. There was no way she was jumping into that dark water, miles below them.

'Maybe this is another invisible bridge thing,' said Epizon hopefully, crouching and feeling the stone lip of the cliff.

'Oh no. Oh no.' Phyleus grabbed Lyssa by the arm. 'Jump! We'll have to jump!' He turned her to face the cavern they'd come from. The waterfall wasn't the source of the sound. A tidal wave of water was flooding towards them.

'There are tunnels here!' shouted Epizon.

Lyssa dropped to her knees at the same time as Phyleus, leaning out over the edge carefully to look where Epizon was pointing. There was a wide lip of rock jutting out a few feet down the cliff face with three dark tunnels disappearing into the rock itself. A glimmer of purple appeared in the mouth of the middle one.

'The light! It's what we're supposed to do next,' she said with relief, and launched herself feet first off the edge of the cliff towards the middle tunnel.

14

EVADNE

Evadne listened as Theseus told Abderos about yet another bloody ship. He couldn't get enough. Endless questions about speed, ballistas, sails, even the galleys. Theseus didn't seem to mind, though, chatting amiably, showing no signs of frustration, worry or fear. She swivelled on her backside, reaching out and touching the ice wall of the cage again. She winced as she did, the material so cold it burned. It was holding against the boar's insistent battering, so far. She estimated that they had been trapped for over an hour, but she couldn't be sure.

'What happened to your legs?' Theseus's question, punctuated by the hammering of the boar against the ice, caught her attention. She turned to Abderos, as did Busiris, who had been sullen and silent since she'd snapped at him. Abderos shifted in his chair, looking down at his hands.

'It was my own fault.'

Theseus said nothing and after a moment Abderos spoke again. 'I grew up on a farm in Gemini,' he said. 'I wanted to fly. I've always wanted to fly, since as long as I can remember. But my parents wanted me to work on the farm.

I would visit the docks whenever I could, at first only looking at the ships, but when I was older I started sneaking on board. The first time I actually flew, nobody knew I was on the ship. I hadn't meant to be on board when they left, but gods, what a thrill.' His eyes lit up at the memory. Evadne cocked her head. He reminded her of how she'd felt about books when she was young. Still felt about books.

'Anyway, we didn't return to Gemini for three days. My parents were out of their minds with worry, and I was starving when I got home. But after that I knew there was no way I was staying on the farm. It was a Crosswind, by the way. My first stowaway experience. I was eight.' His smile faded. 'My second stowaway experience... They caught me. And they took me to Aries.' Evadne looked away, unwanted pity for him growing inside her. 'As you can imagine, an eight-year-old kid didn't do very well in the world of the warriors. The first slaver who bought me put me out as bait for the chimeras in a gladiator show.' She shuddered. 'I lost both legs in one bite from a lion head, and the flames from a dragon head cauterised the wounds. Luckily for me, the second I lost consciousness the beasts left me alone and moved onto still-moving prey. A slaver's wife took pity on me when she realised I was alive after the show, patched up the stumps and my burns and taught me to cook. Lyssa found me five years later. She let me learn to fly the ship. Said I was a natural.'

'How old are you?' asked Theseus softly.

'Sixteen,' he said, the grin back on his face. 'And I'm the best damn navigator in the Trials.'

Theseus barked a short laugh and clapped the arm of the wheelchair. 'I don't doubt it, young Abderos. I don't doubt it.'

Abderos turned to the half-giant. 'What about you, Busiris? How did you end up in the Trials?'

Busiris scowled at him. 'None of your business,' he snapped.

'Hmmmmmm,' said Theseus, giving him a long, appraising look. 'Let's play a game. I'll guess and you tell me if I'm wrong or right.'

Busiris said nothing.

'You speak well,' continued Theseus, 'and I've not seen you keen to fight so far, which is uncommon for a giant. That makes me think you're noble-born.' The half-giant's face twitched. 'And your gold skin. That's native to Egypt, in Aries, isn't it?'

Busiris sighed. 'If you know who I am, little man, then just say it.' The sullen pettiness had been replaced with an arrogant sneer. 'Or no, I will. I am the king of Egypt.' He squared his shoulders. 'And I can fight just fine. I simply prefer to have others do it for me, while I attend to more important matters.'

'Where's Egypt?' asked Evadne, interest piqued. 'I've never heard of it.'

Busiris glared but Theseus said, 'It's in the middle of Aries. It's desert land. Very hot.'

'Is it near the gladiator pits?' asked Abderos, a bit quietly.

'Sort of, yes. The south of Aries is ruled by the Amazonians and is jungle but most of the north is run by slavers. The pits are everywhere.'

'We don't have gladiator shows in Egypt,' barked Busiris. 'We leave that to those barbaric idiots. My armies are organised, and only fight when there is something to be gained.'

'Sounds more like Athena's thing than Aries'. Strategy over brute strength and all that,' said Evadne.

'Are you suggesting that I am weak?'

Evadne looked at him, seeing his black eyes cold behind the heavy liner. She thought about Busiris's crew-mate Eryx, with his fierce allegiance to his captain and his simple courage. Busiris would likely live longer, granted, but she doubted he was as strong-willed or as motivated. Did that make him weak? Maybe she could find out.

'Not at all. Brute strength is nothing without strategy. Why waste energy on a doomed outcome?' She shrugged. Busiris narrowed his eyes at her and grunted,

'How did you end up here?'

'Hercules needed a gunner.'

'That's it? Come on, we're all sharing here. Where are you from?' Abderos said.

'Leo.'

'Nice. Leo's really nice,' he said.

'Yeah.' Leo was really nice, if your parents gave a shit about you, she added silently.

'Lots of money there. Are your family rich?'

Evadne sighed as Abderos asked the question. Her family were rich. And their money was more important than their time or their children. 'You don't need to know about me, or my family. Enough questions,' she said aloud, getting to her feet.

Busiris glared at Abderos.

'Great. You've made her start pacing again,' he growled.

15

HERCULES

'A sterion, jump now!' Hercules roared the last word as the minotaur teetered on the edge of the underground cliff. Animalistic fear was etched into Asterion's face and Hercules bared his teeth as his patience with the creature ran out. He placed a hand on his first-mate's back and pushed. A wild howl erupted from the minotaur as his hooves scrabbled on the ground, then he began to slide down the cliff.

Hercules glanced at the tidal wave fast approaching them, then over the edge of the precipice as Asterion slid into the wide central tunnel, still bellowing unintelligibly. He sat on the edge and pushed himself off, into the pipe on the right, the one the dancing white light had disappeared down. He felt a smattering of water over his head as he slid off the cliff, his breath catching at the sudden drop, then he heard the whoosh of water as the wave flooded over the edge of the cliff, creating a mirror of the waterfall opposite and cascading over him and the tunnel. Within seconds he was plunged into darkness, a cold trickle of water beneath him as he raced through the pitch-black pipe. He could no longer hear Asterion's howls as he sped through the tunnel, his momentum carrying him up the smooth cold sides as he rounded bend after tight bend. He took long measured breaths, hoping to see the guiding white light ahead of him at any minute, but the tunnel stayed dark as the trickle of water beneath him grew.

HERCULES SWIRLED around the inside of the mountain in the slowly flooding tunnel for what felt like eternity. He knew he didn't need to panic, there was no way Apollo would devise an obstacle that couldn't be beaten, but he was starting to feel nauseous in the endless dark, with no idea where his body would be thrown next. The water was now halfway up his hips and although the impenetrable lion hide protected his backside from the constant sliding it couldn't stop the freezing liquid from washing up his legs to his crotch. Suddenly the tunnel opened out and Hercules barely stopped himself crying out as he was launched from the pipe into a dimly lit cavern. He flailed his arms as he fell with an almighty splash into a freezing pool. Kicking hard, adrenaline coursing through him, he righted himself under the water and broke back through the surface. He gulped down air, acutely aware of the weight of the wet lion skin and massive sword fighting against his attempts to stay on the surface.

'Captain!' He kicked himself round in a circle, looking for Asterion. The minotaur was swimming towards him, making significantly fewer waves than he was. He tried to calm himself. He didn't need Asterion to see him out of control. 'The cavern is going to flood.'

Hercules looked around the cavern properly. It was lit by the same blue flames within chunks of ice in the carved walls. There were three tunnels allowing water to pour into the cave, and no other ways in or out that he could see.

'If those are the tunnels we came in from, how do we get out?' he demanded as the minotaur reached him.

'We must have to go down,' Asterion replied.

Hercules frowned. The water had risen a foot in the short time they had been in the cavern. He took a deep breath and ducked his head under the ice-cold water, feeling his skin tighten as the cold enveloped him. He swivelled his head, trying to take in as much as he could through the dark water. There was the light! Maybe ten feet below them, hovering. He pushed his head back up.

'The light is down there. Let's go,' he said, before taking another massive breath and diving down. The cold water stung his eyes as he kicked his way down towards the white light, brightening as he approached it. He was expecting to see another tunnel in the rock, a way out of the cavern, but he didn't. Instead he saw a blue circle, pulsing and glowing. The white light bumped gently against it.

Hercules's eyebrows knitted together and he reached out towards the circle. As he touched it, it changed colour, to bright white. The guiding light danced away from the circle, zipping across the pool in the other direction. As Hercules removed his hand from the circle to follow the light it immediately turned blue again. He propelled himself through the water after the light, until he reached the other side of the cavern and a second glowing blue circle. He pushed his hand against it and waited. Nothing happened. The light bounced for a moment, then zipped off again.

Hercules needed more air. In two big strokes of his strong arms he was back at the surface. He took a big breath, then dived back down, looking for the light. He found it, still ten feet down and hovering in the middle of the pool. When he reached it, it zoomed off again, this time straight down. Hercules kicked after it, his ears popping as he went deeper. Soon he could see the floor of the pool. The only thing clear on the dark rock was a third pulsing circle. With a big kick he reached out and touched it, turning it white. Still nothing happened. He waited until his lungs began burning for air, then kicked angrily back to the surface.

'What am I supposed to do?' he shouted over the now-roaring sound of the water cascading into the fast-filling cavern.

'I don't know, Captain,' Asterion answered, treading water. 'What is the light showing you to do?'

'Touch all the circles! I've done that!' Hercules gave an involuntary shiver. The freezing water was starting to take its toll, his powerful legs tiring sooner than they should. Touch all the circles... What if he needed to touch all three at the same time? There was only him and Asterion.

'Asterion, dive down to the blue circle over there and hold your hand on it, on my mark,' he barked. Asterion nodded and took a breath. 'Go!' They both kicked under the water again, Hercules moving swiftly to the blue circle opposite the one Asterion was headed to. He pressed his hand to it and waited a second before a low rumbling sounded. He looked down, trying to see through the dark water and noticed the current changing, pulling down-wards. A section of the floor, right in the centre, was moving up towards them. He watched, hovering in place as a disc of the stone floor rose higher, and water was sucked down into the hole left in the floor beneath, easily big enough for him to pass through. The disc stopped suddenly, then began moving back down again, water rushing back up towards the surface. He let go of the circle and swam to the surface. Asterion was there already, gasping.

'I can't hold my breath that long,' he wheezed.

'Idiot,' Hercules hissed. The water level had risen higher than the lowest tunnel now, leaving only about four feet of air above them. 'We'll have to hold on as long as we can, then the second we let go of the circles, dive for the hole at the bottom.'

'Yes, Captain.' Apprehension danced in the beast's bull eyes.

'This is our only chance, Asterion. If you screw this up we both die.' Hercules projected every ounce of malice he possessed into the threat. Asterion nodded.

'Go.'

AGAIN THEY DUCKED under the water, moving faster this time to the blue circles. The disc in the floor began to rise like a plug being lifted, the water rushing down past Hercules and making the lion-skin cloak ripple. He watched carefully, and as soon as he judged the disc high enough for him to make his escape he launched himself towards the hole. He kicked hard, tapping his reserves of strength, determined to get there before Asterion. The disc was dropping, but not as fast as he was swimming. His ears popped again as he reached the black hole, gripped the edge and pulled himself through it.

16

ERYX

Eryx burst from the freezing water, his lungs burning in his wounded chest as he gulped down crisp air. Bergion splashed to the surface beside him, heaving and retching as he forced air into his own lungs.

'Where's Antaeus?' Eryx gasped. Bergion shook his head and Eryx's heart faltered. Then an almighty splash on his other side rocked him in the water and he kicked frantically to turn himself around. Antaeus only surfaced long enough to look desperately at Eryx, his skin deathly pale, before he sank back under the water, arms limp. Eryx swore, took a big breath and dived back under the water after his captain. The giant was sinking fast, his weight dragging him down towards the hole they had just emerged from, but Eryx moved faster, gripping Antaeus's wrist and pulling hard.

Antaeus had become a dead weight, his eyes glassy. Fear filled Eryx and he pulled harder, enough to stop the giant's descent but not enough to get him back to the surface. Frustration welled inside him as he wrapped his other hand around Antaeus's wrist and pulled, his kicks futile.

Suddenly, Bergion was there, his dark form and long beard clear under the water. He gripped Antaeus's other wrist and then they were moving up, fast. They broke the surface as one and Eryx scanned his surroundings. They were in another lake, but this one was in a gloomy forest, dark willows branching out from a grassy bank ten feet away. He grunted as he kicked for the closest shore, turning constantly to check Antaeus's lifeless head was out of the water. Between them they scrabbled onto dry land, hauling their captain with them. Panic rushed in as Eryx looked at him, not knowing if the blue skin was due to cold or lack of air.

'What do we do?'

Bergion said nothing as he kneeled beside Antaeus, unclipped his cloak and held his own ear to the giant's chest. After a moment he wriggled one massive arm under Antaeus's back and pulled him up into a sitting position.

'Hold him here,' he grunted. Eryx did as he was told, kneeling behind his captain to hold his gigantic frame up. Bergion took a deep breath, then punched Antaeus squarely in the chest.

'What are you doing!' yelled Eryx, shocked, but Bergion ignored him, moving back and then punching him again. Antaeus shuddered under his hands. Bergion punched a third time and Antaeus heaved, throwing water up as he lurched forward. Bergion backed away quickly and Eryx leaped to his feet.

'Captain! Are you all right?'

'Does he look all right?' snapped Bergion. Antaeus continued to heave, his breath rattling as he panted, but the colour was returning to his face.

'How did you know what to do?' asked Eryx quietly, awed.

'Albion and I used to drown each other sometimes.' Bergion shrugged. Eryx stared at him, infinitely glad both that he hadn't been brought up in the same way as a full giant and that he'd never had a brother.

A gentle cooing sounded overhead and Eryx looked up, into the trees.

This was not a normal forest, he realised.

17

LYSSA

'Get down, the phoenix is back!'

Lyssa dropped to the ground the second she heard Epizon hiss the warning. Her still-wet clothes squelched beneath her as she lay flat against the forest floor. If you could call it a forest. There were no trees like these anywhere else in Olympus, she was sure. They glowed with all the colours of a diamond: ice blues, bright purples and soft teals. Each leaf looked like a glistening gem and there was an eerie absence of the noises she'd expect in a forest. There were no rustling leaves, birdsong, tapping of critters' feet or murmurs of wind through trees. Under normal circumstances she would have found it very beautiful, peaceful even, but having nearly drowned in the last cavern, she was in no place to appreciate it. She was angry. If Epizon hadn't suggested they try touching the circles all at once, their lungs would have filled with ice-cold water and that would have been the end. The end of her chance to stop Hercules, the end of the Trials. The end of her life. Worse, the end of Abderos, Epizon and Phyleus's lives too. She would have been responsible for killing most of her crew.

Nausea coiled in her belly and she clenched her teeth, forcing her Rage to replace it. This was Apollo's fault, not hers. He took Abderos, he designed a bunch of traps to try to kill them. Athena made her do this, made her risk her and her crew's lives to do what the goddess herself couldn't and prevent a lunatic from living forever. Her muscles twitched as she lay flat on the ground, shaking with both cold and anger.

'I think it's gone,' Phyleus whispered loudly.

'I've had enough of this,' she spat as she jumped to her feet. Phyleus was standing up slowly, brushing gently glimmering leaves from his soggy clothes.

'Yeah, I think we all have,' he muttered.

'I mean it. I've had enough of being used, pushed around, forced to—' A heavy hand came to rest on her shoulder. She tensed but closed her mouth.

'This is not the time, or the place, Captain,' Epizon said and stepped in front of her. 'We need to focus on Abderos. We can discuss the gods later.' The warning was clear on his face. *The world is watching.* She closed her eyes and took a breath. As she did, music began. Her eyes flew open, taking in Epizon's surprise.

'Where...?' She trailed off.

It was the most incredible sound she'd ever heard. She knew, all at once, that there was nothing wrong with the world. Nothing wrong with her, or with her crew, or with the gods. Everybody was fine. Better than fine. They were happy. She was happy. A slow smile spread across her face and Epizon barked out a laugh.

'Isn't it amazing?' he muttered.

'It is,' she agreed and sat down on the cold earth. She was dimly aware of a bright blue bird beating its wings high above them, a moment of blissful cold enveloping her, wrapping her up safely. The melody continued, light and dancing, happy and hopeful. If she just stayed here she would be fine. They all would.

'LYSSA!' A loud voice broke through her serenity. 'Lyssa, listen to me, we have to go.' The voice was urgent, and it didn't go with the pretty music. She frowned.

'Phyleus?'

'Yes, Lyssa, you have to cover your ears. Come on,' he said and tried to pull her to her feet. He had one arm wrapped around his head, trying to cover both ears at once. She looked at Epizon, sitting beside her. He shrugged.

'Why don't you want to listen to this lovely music?'

'It's phoenix song, and you'll die if you stay here. We need to go. We need to rescue Abderos.' *Abderos*. The name jarred her, like the wrong note had been hit in the tune. 'Lyssa, please.'

'Captain,' she said, without thinking. 'It's *Captain*.' A smile crossed Phyleus's worried face and he tugged on her arm hard.

'Yes. Yes, it is. Captain, we need to go and rescue Abderos, before we run out of time.'

It all came back to her in such a rush she gasped. She pulled out of Phyleus's grip and clapped her hands over her ears, fighting the peaceful feeling still lingering, pulling at her consciousness. Her Rage returned, full force, pulsing through her body so hard it was as though it was making up for being lulled to sleep. She snarled. Phyleus took a nervous step back from her.

'How do we kill it?' she growled.

'We don't. If you kill a phoenix it will be reborn and you'll have an enemy for life,' Phyleus answered. More questions swam through her mind as Epizon looked up at her placidly. She reached for his arm.

'We've got to go,' she said to him. He nodded and stood up obligingly. Phyleus rolled his eyes.

'If you weren't so stubborn I could have got you to do that,' he muttered as he turned away. She scowled at him, her hands back over her ears, her adrenaline pushing her through the piercing cold the phoenix was beating down at them.

'Well, why dddddidn't it affect you? And how do you know so mmmuch abbbout phoenixes?' Her teeth were chattering as she started to jog, away from the pool and the bird, turning often to make sure Epizon was following.

'I ddddid tell you I knew pppplenty about Olympus, and you chose not to bbbelieve me,' he snarked, jogging beside her.

'Why didn't it affect you?' she asked again. The cold was lessening as they got further from the bird and she was sure the glowing plants around them were getting brighter.

'I'm...' Phyleus started but didn't finish. She looked sideways at him as she ran, moving faster as warmth returned to her limbs and power surged around her body. She didn't have time to ask more questions. Looming ahead of them, rising from the ground and growing as they neared it, was an enormous gladiator pit carved from ice.

18

EVADNE

'So, what *do* you do on the *Orion*?'

Evadne slumped down next to Busiris. He scowled at her, as she had expected him to. 'I know you're first mate,' she continued as she folded her legs beneath her on the hard ground, 'but what does that actually mean you do? Eryx won the Hydra Trial, didn't he?' She raised her eyebrows at the giant as he snorted.

'Eryx is not worthy of first mate.'

'How come Antaeus seems to give him all the good jobs, then?'

'He gives him the jobs that need blind strength. I told you, I prefer to make my moves with some consideration.'

Evadne looked at him thoughtfully. 'What's it like to be a king?' she asked.

'Not as good as it will be to be an immortal king,' he answered. For the first time, she saw a smile pulling at his mouth.

'Do your people like you?'

'Well enough,' He shrugged, then narrowed his black eyes at her. His face was twice the size of her own and his gold skin shone against their icy background. 'Why do you ask so many questions?'

Evadne shrugged too.

'There's a lot to learn about Olympus.' She nodded at Theseus and Abderos, still talking about ships. 'I'm far more interested in lands and kings than I am in ships. Does everyone in Egypt have gold skin?'

'Most. Not all. The sun burns skin in my desert.'

'Are you cold now?' He shook his head. 'I am,' she muttered. Then she asked, as casually as she could, 'Have you met Poseidon?'

Busiris's face instantly hardened.

'No,' he spat.

'What about when he asked the crew to be his heroes?'

'He asked Antaeus, and Antaeus came to me. I have never shared words with my father.'

It was interesting that Poseidon had so little interest in most of his sons. What was different about Antaeus, she wondered.

'So, you're in this for the eternal life, rather than fame or glory in your father's name?'

'Eternal life is worth far more than fame or glory,' he said quietly.

Evadne cocked her head. 'Fame and glory *are* a kind of immortality,' she said.

'Pah,' he barked, dismissing the statement with a sweep of his massive hand. 'Metaphors and philosophy. We're being offered the real thing. True immortality. A chance to live forever.' His fist clenched as he spoke, his hard eyes gleaming with intensity. So, Evadne thought, Busiris was very motivated indeed. Just as motivated as Eryx in fact, just not by loyalty or pride.

. . .

'LOOK!' Abderos's voice broke through their conversation, and he pointed at the wall of the cage. The surface was shimmering and fluctuating, then it hardened, showing them an image. Theseus sat up straight, alert. It was Psyche, Bellerephon and Hedone, all running up a narrow spiral staircase that looked like it was made of glass. Wet cloaks flapped behind them as they ran, glimpses of Psyche's golden armour gleaming beneath hers. All four prisoners watched in silence as the team burst from the staircase onto a long promenade. Abderos breathed in sharply.

'Gladiator pit,' he whispered. He was right, Evadne thought as she stood up slowly. Psyche was leading her crew along a curved bench meant as seating for the audience at fights. Suddenly there was an almighty *crack* and her attention was ripped from the image to the other side of the cage. The side the boar was attacking. A splinter had appeared in the ice, at head height. Busiris shifted on the ground and she stepped quickly over his leg and reached out her hand. As she did so the splinter grew, cracking as it lengthened. The snorts of the boar seemed louder as she watched it back up, distorting through the ice wall. They were nearly out of time.

19

HEDONE

Hedone panted as they sprinted along the bench seats after the red light. They had gladiator pits like this in Pisces but they were mostly used to host plays and concerts. She glanced sideways, to where a huge cube of ice sat in the centre of the pit, being battered repeatedly by a boar taller than she was. Theseus was in there.

Her stomach constricted and her heart fluttered before the thought was replaced with, *At least Hercules wasn't in there*. She realised Psyche was slowing down and reduced her own pace with relief. Her wet clothes were weighing her down, making every stride harder. She'd always loved to swim but after that cavern filling up she'd not be doing it again in a while. She didn't know how Psyche had done it, swimming with all that armour on. She felt hot from exertion and cold from her wet clothes and the frigid air, her sweat indistinguishable from water now.

'I think this is it,' breathed Psyche as they reached a column of ice jutting up from the bench. It was sheer and stretched up into the sky and the whole thing pulsed gently with red light. There was a dark hole in the front of the column, easily ten feet above their heads.

'What do we do?' asked Bellerephon. Psyche slipped her pack off her shoulder and pulled it open.

'I guess it has something to do with this,' she answered, pulling out the red metal sphere Apollo had dropped onto their ship at the start. 'Apollo said it was a key.'

'You reckon that hole is the lock?' Bellerephon gestured at the hole in the column.

'Let's give it a go,' said Psyche. She hefted the sphere in one hand, aiming, then threw. The sphere hit the column a few inches under the hole and clattered loudly to the ice bench at their feet. Hedone dropped into a crouch quickly, retrieving it before it could roll away. She handed it back to Psyche. 'Want a go?' the woman asked her.

Hedone shook her head immediately. If Psyche didn't have the strength to get the sphere high enough, she certainly wouldn't. Bellerephon took it from her instead and took only a second to aim before launching it at the column. Hedone's mouth dropped open as it sailed straight into the hole and a whirring sound started up. Psyche clapped him hard on the back and he shrugged, grinning.

Then, with a flash of red light, Theseus was sitting on the bench next to them. He blinked rapidly, then scrabbled to his feet.

'Thank the gods for that,' he said and, grasped Psyche's outstretched hand. She smiled at him, and Hedone could see clearly that it was an adoration different to her own. It was respect.

'Who was rescued first?' Psyche asked, eyes gleaming. Theseus looked around at them all, a broad smile slowly taking over his handsome face.

'Me. You did it. We won.'

20

LYSSA

L yssa hated spiral staircases. They were too narrow and made her legs feel a bit wobbly at the best of times. Being able to see the distorted ground through steps made of ice wasn't helping.

'Nearly there,' panted Phyleus behind her. She rolled her eyes. He had no idea if they were nearly there. She supposed saying it helped him keep going.

Abruptly the staircase did end, funnelling them out into one of the rows of bench seats surrounding the pit. Her breath caught as a loud clang rang through the structure. It was the massive boar, slamming into a cube made of ice in the middle of the pit. She started to move down the rows, towards the cage, but Epizon called out to her.

'Captain! The light.'

She looked up to see him pointing. The purple light they had followed so far was bouncing along the row of seats, towards a sheer column also glowing purple. She sighed angrily as she climbed back up the benches, then jogged along after the light. It was clear what they had to do when they got there. There was a hole in the column, just a little bigger than the key Apollo had given them, a few feet above Epizon's head. She fished the sphere out of her pack and took a few long strides. Both men moved backwards, out of her way.

She took a long breath and dropped her stance. She let loose the Rage coiled in her muscles and ran, focusing on Abderos's face. As she reached the column she jumped and stretched her arm high. The sphere weighed nothing in her hand and she threw it easily, aiming for the hole. It hit the column a little high, then dropped and caught on the bottom edge of the hole, tipping into the darkness. Relief flooded Lyssa as she landed back on her feet. A whirring sound echoed around them, then, with a flash of purple light, Abderos was there, chair and all, beside them.

HE BARKED A LAUGH, eyes wide with astonishment as he looked at them. Lyssa threw her arms around him, eyes blurring. She dashed angrily at the tears she couldn't help. She'd not let herself consider that she might actually lose him, but now he was here the relief was so strong it was making her head pound and her heart hammer. Abderos had been a child when she found him. He was the closest thing to a little brother she had, since Hercules had taken her actual brother. She screwed her eyes shut tightly, hoping nobody would notice her crying.

'Thanks, Cap,' Abderos said into her wet hair. 'Shame you weren't a few minutes earlier.' She pushed back from him, opening her eyes and raising her eyebrows in question. 'Theseus was rescued not five minutes ago. He's a nice guy, by the way. Turns out he doesn't have a swimming pool, though.'

Phyleus laughed and clapped him on the shoulder. 'That's a shame,' he said.

'Yeah, but it makes sense, I mean, how would you fit a pool onto—'

'I meant that we didn't win,' Phyleus cut him off.

'Oh. Yeah. But I didn't get eaten by a boar so...' He gave a small shiver and Lyssa let out a long breath. She suspected he didn't feel as casual about his rescue as he was making out, but he was safe. That was what mattered most. It was an added bonus that Hercules hadn't won.

21

HERCULES

Hercules got the sphere into the hole on his second try. At the first attempt he'd used too much force, the sphere bouncing off the column and into the rows of benches below them. After Asterion had retrieved it he had tried again, moderating his strength this time. There was a whirring sound and a flash of white light and then Evadne was standing in the row with them, confusion written across her face.

'What...?' she stammered, then her face sagged in relief and she sat down hard on the bench behind her. 'The boar was almost through,' she breathed.

'Were we first?' Hercules demanded. Evadne dropped her gaze to the ground, and shook her head.

'Theseus,' she said quietly. Hercules's fist lashed out, hitting the column.

'All that, for nothing!' he shouted. Evadne frowned, opening her mouth, then closing it again. 'Do you know what I've been through?' he hissed at her. She looked him up and down, taking in his wet clothes.

'I guess it involved water,' she said. He stepped towards

her, his temper flashing and she shifted away from him quickly.

'Busiris is still in the cage,' she said. 'And the boar is almost through the ice.'

'How is that relevant to me?' Hercules hissed.

'I think we may be able to use him.' Evadne pushed her chin out. 'I spoke to him while we were in there. He has little allegiance to his captain and is only driven by becoming immortal. Turns out he's a king of some place called Egypt.'

Hercules had heard of Egypt. It was deep in Aries, a tough place by all accounts. A king might be a useful ally to have. He scowled at Evadne.

'How does that help me if he's eaten by a boar?'

'We could help him. Then he would be indebted to us.'

Hercules laughed loudly. Had she gone mad? She wanted to help their opponents?

'You want me to rescue your new friend?' he asked incredulously. She folded her arms.

'A half-giant king with lands and wealth is the sort of person you want to owe you a debt,' she said coolly.

'Or the sort of person *you* might try to win over yourself,' he hissed, his eyes narrowing. All it took was two hours alone with a half-giant and Evadne had turned her eyes elsewhere. That would not do.

'Captain, I just think it—'

'Don't,' he spat, cutting her off. 'Don't think, don't speak, don't do anything except sit there and watch your new boyfriend get ripped to pieces.'

22

ERYX

They weren't going to make it. The realisation made Eryx sick to his stomach. Escaping the ice phoenix a second time had been too much for Antaeus. The giant was barely responsive and so cold to touch. Eryx was exhausted from helping to drag him through the forest, his wet boots rubbing sores on his feet and his injured chest aching deeply.

HE WOULDN'T ACTUALLY MISS Busiris, but he didn't want him to be eaten by a giant boar. He didn't think anybody deserved that. A giant like his captain might have stood a chance against it, but Busiris was not a fighter.

'Captain won't be happy if Busiris gets eaten,' grunted Bergion, voicing Eryx's own thoughts. Eryx couldn't see the giant past Antaeus's limp form but he nodded anyway.

'We might still make it,' he said.

'We've been out here over two hours.'

They lapsed into silence again, trudging past the

sparkling trees and plants. 'Least it's Busiris, though,' Bergion said. 'Wouldn't like it to be Albion.'

It was the nicest thing Eryx had ever heard either brother say about the other. A small smile tugged at his lips.

'Yeah. That would be bad,' he agreed.

'Hope Antaeus makes it, though. If Antaeus dies and Busiris lives, he'll be captain.

Eryx scowled. He hadn't thought of that. 'Course Antaeus'll make it. He's the strongest man I've ever met.'

'He's the heaviest,' Bergion grunted in response.

23

HEDONE

'Y ou want us to do what?' Hedone saw Captain Lyssa frowning at Theseus as he spoke to her.

Hedone herself was aching. Her whole body was cold, cold like she'd never felt before. She'd never physically exerted herself so much in her life, and the short run round the circular pit to where the crew of the *Alastor* were gathered around their purple column had been the final straw. She couldn't do any more. She slumped backwards, onto the bench.

'I want you to help me get Busiris out of there,' Theseus repeated slowly. 'Psyche and Bellerephon will provide cover, I'll distract the boar and you break into the cage.'

'Firstly, why? And secondly, are we even allowed to do that?' Lyssa said.

Theseus shrugged. 'It's not right to leave him to die. And if it's not allowed, what will they do? They can't kill off two heroes this early.' He grinned and Hedone saw Lyssa's face soften. She knew the power of that man's smile.

'Fine,' said Lyssa after a moment.

'Excellent,' said Theseus and vaulted over the bench

below them towards the cage. Psyche kneeled beside Hedone quickly.

'Are you all right?' The concern in Psyche's voice surprised her.

'I'm just tired. And cold,' she said.

'You need to keep moving, or the cold will set in properly. Stay here, though,' Psyche said, then straightened up and pulled out her slingshot as she followed Theseus. Hedone forced herself to her feet, wincing at the squelch of her wet boots. She didn't watch as Lyssa and her captain raced to save the half-giant, though. She scanned the benches of the pit instead, looking for the other columns. Her eyes landed on the white column, and the massive form of Hercules beside it. She knew, somehow, that he would not help rescue Busiris. And she couldn't work out how she felt about it. She knew that he *should* help. She knew that she would, if she could. But somehow, she understood. It was obvious to her why he must let his opponents die. What kind of a competition would it be otherwise? He needed to win and Hedone would do anything to see him gain an immortal life. He looked towards her and her breath caught. Their eyes locked across the pit and fire burned within her. She would do anything for him.

24

EVADNE

E vadne tried to keep her face impassive as she watched Lyssa and Theseus get closer to the floor of the pit. Hercules was a fool not to listen to her. Allies were necessary now; they were four Trials in and had only one victory. They had no chance of a treaty with Lyssa, obviously, and while Hercules seemed interested in Hedone, it was unlikely Theseus would oblige. The giants had been their best bet and this was a perfect opportunity. A question clawed at her, and she did not want to admit she already knew the answer. *Would Hercules have saved me, if he knew he had already lost the Trial?* She'd seen no relief on his face to see her safe. Yet the others were risking their lives to save somebody who wasn't even on their crew.

A SQUEAL FROM the boar below caught her attention and she leaned forward on her bench. Psyche was standing on a seat five or six rows up from the floor, her slingshot drawn and her gold armour gleaming. A ripple of admiration ran through Evadne as she watched the woman aim again, unwavering and solid. She heard a shout and as the boar snorted and kicked under Psyche's pellets she saw Theseus waving his arms a few feet from the cage. The boar saw him too and dropped its head, its massive curving tusks scraping the ground as it drew it hooves across the ice. Then it lurched forward after Theseus and he whirled around, running for the benches.

A flash of red hair by the cage caught Evadne's eye and she leaned out further as Lyssa threw her shoulder against the cage. Smashing sounds echoed around the pit as the cage shattered and Busiris leaped to his feet in the middle of the wreckage. Evadne could see the confusion on his large face as he looked around for his crew-mates. He saw Lyssa and she could tell that the girl was saying something to him. Then, out of nowhere, the boar came charging through the shattered ice. Lyssa dived out of the way, rolling and coming up on her feet to sprint towards the benches, but Busiris was not so quick. He jumped aside, avoiding the first charge, but the boar wheeled around, steam erupting from its giant nostrils. It ducked its head again, ready to charge, and Busiris looked from side to side with panicked eyes.

'Run, you fool!' bellowed Theseus. The half-giant seemed to snap back to life at the order, his long legs starting to move. At the same time there was an ear-piercing squeal from the boar and it dropped to the ground, legs folding beneath it. Bellerephon had joined Psyche and they were firing and reloading pellets faster than Evadne would have thought possible.

'Enough!' A voice boomed across the pit. The boar vanished with a whimper and Evadne stood up, holding her breath.

Apollo appeared in the centre of the pit. He was wearing

a white toga and his golden hair flopped onto his forehead as he gave a little bow. He was stunning, she thought, taking an involuntary step towards him. Hercules growled beside her.

'Heroes! What a controversial ending! Oh, but wait, we are missing some competitors.' Apollo waved his hand and Antaeus appeared on the floor of the pit, apparently unconscious and being held up by one of the black-skinned giants and Eryx. They were both so startled they immediately dropped their captain. 'You needn't worry, sons of Poseidon,' Apollo told them. 'The crews of the *Alastor* and the *Virtus* saved your crew-mate from my ravenous pet.' They both dropped to their knees and bowed their heads. 'I'll have to think about whether or not I'll allow that. In the meantime, Theseus! Your crew rescued you first – you are the winner!' Theseus bowed low to the god. 'I think that makes it one win to all four of you. Excellent,' Apollo beamed, exuding youthful energy. 'Couldn't have asked for better. Your next Trial is in two days, and you need to get to Taurus. I'm looking forward to it!' he exclaimed, and vanished.

Two DAYS? A grateful feeling washed over Evadne. Two days to rest. Two days to read and plan.

'Let's go,' Hercules spat, and the tone of his voice made her shiver. Two days to avoid her captain.

25

LYSSA

'I t was the right thing to do, Cap. I mean, he was pretty grumpy but apparently he's a king. And nobody should get eaten by a boar,' Abderos said as he wheeled himself across the deck of the *Alastor*.

'Yeah, well. I just hope Apollo decides to let us carry on.'

'He will,' said Epizon.

'Ever the optimist,' muttered Lyssa, rolling her eyes. She turned to Phyleus. 'You're quiet,' she said. Epizon had been right about giving him a chance. So far he had proved extremely useful and she knew she should acknowledge it.

'Yeah,' he said, not meeting her eyes. She frowned.

'What's wrong?'

'I, er...' He looked up at her. His face was pale and his usually cocky expression was nowhere to be seen. Lyssa stopped walking. He took a deep breath. 'I knew this was coming. I need to tell you something.'

Lyssa's stomach muscles clenched. It was clearly nothing good.

'Go on...' she said, through slightly gritted teeth.

'I haven't been completely honest about who I am,' he said.

Epizon and Abderos had stopped too.

'Nobody on this ship is defined by their past, Phyleus,' Lyssa said, trying to squash her building apprehension. 'I haven't pushed you about where you come from or who you are because I don't care.'

'Well, you might soon.'

Understanding dawned slowly on Lyssa. 'You're from Taurus,' she said slowly. 'And we're going there next.' He fixed his eyes on hers and nodded. 'You told me you didn't know what a bloody maenad was! They're native to Taurus,' she snapped.

'I know, I'm sorry for lying to you. I just... I just wanted to prove myself without you having any idea who I am.'

'Why? Who are you?'

The ship suddenly pitched forward violently and Lyssa gasped as she was thrown to the deck. She pushed herself back up fast, muscles burning as her power sprang to life. Nestor was galloping across the deck towards her.

'Captain, we're under attack!'

DIONYSUS

THE IMMORTALITY TRIALS

TRIAL FIVE

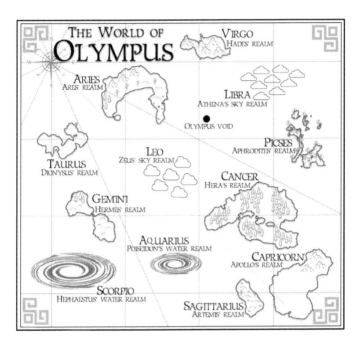

The World of
Olympus

VIRGO
Hades' realm

ARIES
Ares' realm

LIBRA
Athena's sky realm

● Olympus void

PICSES
Aphrodites' realm

LEO
Zeus' sky realm

TAURUS
Dionysus' realm

CANCER
Hera's realm

GEMINI
Hermes' realm

AQUARIUS
Poseidon's water realm

CAPRICORN
Apollo's realm

SCORPIO
Hephaestus' water realm

SAGITTARIUS
Artemis' realm

1

LYSSA

L yssa whirled around as she found her footing, looking for the source of the attack. Beyond the gleaming sails of the *Alastor* she could see the huge, looming form of Lady Lamia's Zephyr drifting towards them, ballistas aimed. The *Alastor* rocked again but although she stumbled Lyssa stayed on her feet as she raced towards the mast, ready to pour her power into the ship.

'They're coming alongside, Captain,' shouted Epizon. As he said it Lyssa saw huge metal claws on the end of thick cord ropes slam into the wood of the *Alastor's* deck. She winced as though she could feel the pain of those claws in her own flesh.

'We can still outrun them,' she called back to her first mate.

'The Zephyr's twice our size, Captain, and those are decent ropes.' He had already run to one of the claws and was pulling hard at it, his face straining as he tried to remove the metal from the wood. Nestor was at another claw trying to do the same, bashing the metal repeatedly with a small hammer she'd pulled from her belt. Lyssa wheeled towards the farthest claw even as more sank into the deck. She roared with frustration as she pulled against it, the metal bending beneath her strong hands. Energy and power rushed around her body, feeding her muscles and fuelling her strength.

As she ripped the claw free from the *Alastor* she drew her arm back, ready to launch it at the Lady Lamia's ship, and was shocked to see the Zephyr only a few feet from their own deck. There, with her hood up and her face hidden, was the lady herself, standing under the enormous central mast surrounded by cyclopes. Lyssa's stomach muscles constricted as she aimed the claw directly at the woman and hurled it.

As it sailed across the gap towards its target she heard a roar behind her. She turned and watched, her mouth falling open as Nestor held her hammer high above her head, reared up on her back legs, then began to gallop across the deck of the *Alastor* towards the Zephyr. Lyssa stepped forward, about to shout, when the centaur's feet left the wood. Her white-blond hair blew out behind her, her circlet headband catching the light as she sailed through the air and landed hard on her hooves on the Lady Lamia's deck. Two cyclopes stayed with the lady, one batting away the sharp metal claw Lyssa had thrown, the rest swarming towards the centaur. Before Lyssa could even reach the railings of her own ship Nestor had swung her hammer straight through the heads of three of them. She roared repeatedly as she fought, arms flashing, hair swinging and legs kicking. Lyssa could only gape at the whirlwind of destruction in front of her.

'What the...?' Len breathed beside her, his mouth hanging equally wide open.

'Shouldn't we go and rescue her?' asked Phyleus from Lyssa's other side. She shrugged.

'Doesn't look like she needs rescuing.'

Lady Lamia barked something, then more cyclopes thudded onto the deck from each end of the huge ship. Nestor roared as they closed in on her, disappearing underneath the mob of one-eyed brutes.

Lyssa grabbed the railing, one leg already up and ready to jump when the huddle of cyclopes parted. Nestor was kneeling on her front legs, her back legs bowed, with ropes wrapped tightly around her arms and chest. Two cyclopes were pushing their weight down on her shoulders, forcing her front half to stay low to the ground. Lady Lamia floated past the bleeding and broken guards scattered on the deck towards the *Alastor*, stopping just a few feet from the railings.

'Captain Lyssa,' she said.

'Lady Lamia,' answered Lyssa, stepping back down. She didn't bow her head in respect.

'I believe you have something that belongs to me.'

'She belongs to nobody,' said Epizon, his words ringing clearly across the gap. The Lady Lamia shifted, the movement barely perceptible under the layers of flowing silk.

'She?'

'He or she doesn't matter; it is sentient and therefore cannot be bought or sold.'

'I'll make this very simple for you,' said the lady, her voice silky smooth and her red lips shining through the veil. 'You give me the tank and I'll give you back your centaur.' Lyssa snarled as a guard shoved Nestor's head down further.

'Leave me, Captain,' called Nestor gravely. 'It is my own fault I am here.'

'Don't be ridiculous, Nestor,' Lyssa shouted. She closed

her eyes and took a long breath. 'We'll need some time to get the tank up here,' she said to the lady. There was a pause.

'Fine,' came the measured response.

'Epizon, Phyleus, you're with me.' Lyssa marched across the deck towards the hauler without looking at either man.

'Captain, are you sure this is a good idea?' Phyleus muttered as he hurried to keep up with her.

'Shut up,' she hissed back. They rode the hauler down to the cargo deck in silence, each of them taut and alert. When Lyssa stepped out of the hauler her focus immediately fell on Tenebrae, hovering in the centre of the tank, her tail swishing gently and her vivid eyes fixing on the three of them as they started towards her. Lyssa's coiled, tense Rage made moving the tank into the hauler easy; she barely needed the help of the two men. On the way back up to the top deck she could feel her muscles vibrating with unspent power. How dare this woman attack her ship, take her crew hostage, demand ownership of a living, breathing being? Lyssa clenched and unclenched her fists by her sides, trying not to make her deep breaths too obvious. The hauler doors slid open.

'Captain, what if—' Epizon began but Lyssa cut him off.

'What if something like last time happens when we bring her out into the light? I'm banking on it,' she said and pushed the tank out of the hauler.

2

LYSSA

Lyssa watched Tenebrae in the tank as she pushed it out of the hauler, forcing her own expression to remain neutral as she saw the creature's scales start to glow. When the tank was fully out on deck, the gleaming light from the solar sails reflecting off the water, Lyssa stepped backwards, slowly at first, then faster as Tenebrae closed her eyes. Epizon and Phyleus followed suit.

'Well, Lady Lamia?' Lyssa shouted. 'Is this what you want?' She looked towards the Zephyr, now rail to rail with the *Alastor*. Her eyes widened as the lady rose four feet in the air and began to float across the railings. Her gown hung well past where her feet must have been, making her look abnormally tall. Her guards clambered over the railings, trying to keep up with their mistress. Lady Lamia dropped gracefully to the deck of the *Alastor* without a sound, just a few feet in front of the tank. She cocked to her head to one side, the silk veil moving with her.

'Yes,' she said quietly. 'Yes, this is exactly what I want.' She turned to Lyssa. 'Bring the centaur,' she said loudly. A guard trotted back towards the Zephyr, grunting in a language Lyssa did not know.

Epizon coughed behind her and Lyssa's focus snapped to Tenebrae. Her eyes were opening. Every muscle in Lyssa's body tightened, apprehension filling her, doubt in her plan taking over. That room full of columns... She didn't want to go back there. Would closing her own eyes help?

A strangled sound ripped across the deck of the *Alastor* and all eyes fell on Lady Lamia as she crumpled to the floor. She shrieked again, a noise of a kind Lyssa had never heard anybody make before. It sounded like she couldn't breathe, like the scream was being ripped forcibly from her body. Lyssa's eyes darted back to Tenebrae, who was stock still and staring at the lady, her green eyes flashing. Lyssa turned around, needing to check Epizon was OK. He was standing behind her, upright and alert as he always was, his eyes wide. He saw her looking at him.

'Should we help?' he asked quietly.

Lyssa paused, the groans and cries coming from the woman making her skin crawl. 'I don't know,' she said. Movement caught her eye and she looked over as Nestor's hooves landed on the deck. The cyclopes guards clearly didn't know what to do, looking at one another with confusion on their faces. Nestor bared her teeth at one guard who came close to her and he backed off quickly.

'Nestor, you OK?' Lyssa called, looking again at the Lady Lamia's crumpled form.

'Yes, Captain,' came the centaur's reply. Lyssa moved fast, giving the guards little time to compose themselves. She hurtled towards them, roaring as she approached. Two of the six turned and fled, vaulting over the railings back to the Zephyr. Nestor's hammer flew through another's head and before Lyssa reached them a third guard grunted and dropped to the floor as if by magic. She threw a surprised look sideways to see Phyleus aiming a slingshot. As Nestor made short work of the remaining two guards, Lyssa blocked out the wails of the Lady Lamia.

'Get these claws out of my deck!' she yelled. Her skin throbbed as her Rage thrummed through her, the claws offering her little resistance as she ran from one to another, ripping them from the deck. Each new hole, each new patch of splintered wood in her beloved ship, fuelled her anger. The sounds of Lady Lamia's pain became less disturbing. She deserved it. Whatever was happening in her mind, whatever Tenebrae was doing to her, she deserved it.

'That's all of them, Captain,' called Epizon.

'Then get her off my bloody ship!' shouted Lyssa, leaning over the railings and giving the massive Zephyr a shove, making sure it was no longer tethered to the *Alastor*.

'Captain...' Epizon sounded unsure and Lyssa turned to him. He pointed at the Lady Lamia, twitching and convulsing on the wood. Her flowing gown had moved with her thrashing and a solitary limb could be seen among the folds of blue fabric. Lyssa felt her own face distort as she took in the decayed flesh, the charred-looking skin only partially covering rotten muscle and bone.

'I'll do it, Captain,' Nestor said, and without hesitation galloped to the quivering wreck, bent down and scooped her up around the middle, then cantered to the railings and bodily threw her onto her own deck. Lyssa felt the *Alastor* move and at the same time heard Abderos's voice in her head.

'I got it, Cap,' he said and she looked up to see him at the navigation wheel. She nodded at him and they rose. They didn't need speed now. Lady Lamia would not be following them.

3

HERCULES

'W ell? Is the deck clean?' Hercules stood over Evadne, who was on all fours on the top deck. She sat back on her heels and dragged her forearm across her brow, then looked up at him.

'Yes, Captain. The whole deck is clean.' She said it through slightly gritted teeth and Hercules knew she'd still not learned her lesson. Not only had the girl suggested that they help their enemies in the last Trial, she had evaded punishment for giving up before the end of the race for the golden stag. At this rate she would never learn to respect him. She dropped the rag she was holding into the bucket at her side and pushed herself to her feet. 'I'm going to wash,' she said and turned towards the hauler. He shot his hand out, gripping her shoulder, and she cried out in surprise or pain, he wasn't sure which. He spun her around to face him, a thrill running through his body as he saw her expression change from defiance to apprehension.

'Evadne, I think we need to have a little talk.' He took a step towards her and she took a step backwards. He smiled. Energy thrummed through him. 'Do I make you nervous?' She kept her eyes on his and it struck him how unlike Hedone she looked, her lashes nowhere near as thick, her hair not as silken, her skin not as soft, her lips not as full. Why had he been wasting his time with this girl? Why had he even needed her on board in the first place?

His father's words rang through his mind. *Listen to the girl, she can help you.* He knew she was bright, and though he was reluctant to admit it she probably knew more about Olympus than he did due to her habit of reading so much. He realised she still hadn't answered his question. He cocked his head to one side. 'Well?'

She dropped her eyes to the freshly scrubbed deck. 'Yes, Captain. Sometimes.'

'Good. You should be nervous. I keep reminding you how patient I am with you, but you don't seem to be listening. I don't want to hurt you, Evadne, but if you keep defying me you'll leave me with no choice.'

She looked up at him, her eyes earnest. 'But, Hercules—'

He stepped towards her, his hand raised.

'Captain! You will call me *Captain*!' he shouted. She took two steps back this time, her slight frame seeming even smaller as she cowered. He stood straighter, power swelling him.

'I'm sorry, Captain. It's just that I didn't mean to be taken by Apollo. And I thought that Busiris was weak and cowardly when I spoke to him, and the thought of immortality might make him betray his own crew and join us. I thought that might help us win.' She spoke quickly, desperately.

'So you still do not believe that I am strong enough to win this alone?' A deadly calm had crept into Hercules's voice. Evadne shook her head quickly.

'No, no, that's not what I mean at all. I was just looking for a way to give us an edge, that's all.'

'An edge?' Hercules looked at her, considering. If Zeus said he needed her, then he needed her. But he had to disabuse her of this notion that he was not capable of winning the Trials without help. He gripped her throat in a flash, not giving her time to move or react, or even draw breath. He lifted her clean off her feet and took a few long strides, then pinned her to the metal clad fore-mast of the Hybris. She grabbed at his hand with both of her tiny ones, pulling at his fingers, eyes wide and fearful.

'Please, Captain, please,' she spluttered. 'I'm sorry. I'm sorry. I know you don't need any help, I'm sorry.' The sight of her there, so tiny and fragile in his fist, the knowledge that he could squeeze and end her life... It was enough today. It was enough to know that he could do it. He let go and she dropped the two feet to the ground, taking a huge gulp of air.

'You are lucky, Evadne. You are lucky that I am in control of my temper today.' She didn't look up at him. 'Go and wash. Then I'll see you in my chambers in two hours.' This time she did look up at him, and the look in her eyes was different. Submission, he saw with satisfaction.

4

HEDONE

Hedone had to see Hercules. She wasn't sure she'd ever wanted anything so badly in her entire life. She needed to see him. She needed to make sure that he was OK, he hadn't been hurt in the last Trial. There was also a part of her that needed to hear from him, in his own words, why he chose not to help rescue Busiris from the boar. She didn't believe Hercules was a cruel man or that he'd want to see anybody eaten alive by a wild animal and though she thought she understood why he hadn't got involved it would help to hear him say it.

'Please, Theseus. Please take me with you. I've improved so much since I started training with Psyche.' She did her best pout and the corner of Theseus's mouth quirked into a grin.

'Hedone, after five years I think I'm fairly immune to that smile now,' he said. He looked at Psyche. 'Well? Do you think we should take her with us?'

Psyche stabbed her meat with a fork and looked at Hedone across the galley table. 'It's true she's improved,' she said and took a bite of the steak. 'And she did do well on

Capricorn, though that was mostly down to being a good swimmer.' Hedone looked pleadingly at the older woman as she chewed. Psyche swallowed. 'How about a test?' Theseus raised an eyebrow.

'What did you have in mind?' he said.

'A test of skill,' she answered.

'What sort of skill?' Hedone asked, worry creeping into her voice. She'd face the test, of course, whatever it was, but what if she failed? She needed to see Hercules. She needed to be down on Taurus with him in the next Trial.

'Just a test to see how much you've learned since we began.' Psyche gave Hedone a smile, one of her real ones, and she relaxed slightly. 'It'll be fun.'

HEDONE WOLFED down the rest of her food, repeatedly asking Psyche to tell her what kind of test it would be, but the woman refused to budge, telling her nothing. Theseus seemed highly amused by the whole thing, and Bellerephon entirely uninterested, as usual. When they'd all finished eating Psyche told them to wait for her on the top deck.

'So, why so keen to get involved all of a sudden?' asked Theseus when they were alone. She looked sideways at him as they entered the hauler together.

'Isn't that why you brought me to the Trials?' she asked.

Theseus shook his head. 'No. I brought you because of the prize.'

Hedone frowned at him. 'The prize? Immortality?'

Theseus nodded, leaning back casually against the hauler wall as they rose slowly.

'I can't think of many people I'd want to share an immortal life with,' he said, gently. Hedone's heart skipped a beat and for a moment she couldn't breathe. Confusion gripped her and it must have shown on her face because Theseus stepped forward, looking concerned. 'Hedone?'

She shook her head. 'I'm sorry, I... I just didn't realise that's why I was here.'

'You're a good person, Hedone. And Olympus needs good people. Especially if they're going to be immortal.'

Olympus needed her? Not Theseus? Emotions swam through her mind in a jumble. *Hercules*, she thought. She dragged his face to the forefront of her mind and concentrated. She was to live an immortal life with Hercules. That's what this was about for her now. But Theseus... A tiny voice in the back of her mind persisted. *Theseus just said he wants to share an immortal life with you.*

'Well, I'm glad you're getting on with Psyche, anyway,' he said, snapping her out of her spiralling thoughts. 'And it certainly can't hurt to learn some of her skills. I'll admit it's been harder than I thought it would be for you to stay out of the Trials.'

Hedone looked at him, not really hearing his words. 'Right,' she said as the hauler doors slid open. They stepped out onto the deck and made their way in silence to the mast at the prow of the ship, as instructed by Psyche. The Typhoon's low square sails shimmered, reflecting the pink and orange clouds they were gliding past. They waited awkwardly for a few minutes, until Psyche strode towards them holding a bone spear painted with deep blue markings. She reached the mast, saying nothing, and leaned the spear against it as she pulled a small pot out of the pouch on her belt. She wasn't wearing her golden armour, just black fighting leathers, but gold cord gleamed in her dark braids as she opened the pot and dipped her finger in. When she pulled it out it was bright red and she leaned over and drew a big cross on the centre of the thick mast, at a height level with her shoulder. She picked up the spear and took ten measured strides backwards. She positioned her arm, balancing the spear carefully, focusing on the cross on the mast, then threw. The spear pierced the centre of the cross and Psyche smiled at Hedone.

'Your turn,' she said. Hedone's heart sank. She was getting better with a slingshot but the spears were heavy and she didn't have the strength to lift them high or throw them far. Her aim wasn't too bad over a small distance but unless she was supposed to hit the floor she didn't think this would go well.

She walked unenthusiastically towards Psyche, who shook her head. 'Go and get the spear first,' she said.

Hedone sighed and changed direction. She struggled just to yank the spear out of the wood. Eventually she ripped it free and made her way to where Psyche was standing. The mast seemed very far away. She rolled her shoulders and tried to focus, remembering what Psyche had taught her about throwing on the exhale, looking to where you wanted the weapon to go and making sure you were using your leading eye. She hefted the bone spear, reluctant to lift it higher than her shoulder until she needed to, to save her muscles.

She shifted around until she felt like she had her stance correct, then drew her arm back. If she wanted to get the distance and the height she would need to get enough momentum. Enough strength.

Hercules was strong. She could draw from his strength. A memory of their hour together flashed through her mind. His strength mingling with hers, his power inside her, part of her. She drew her arm back a little further and threw. The spear sailed towards the mast and Hedone's mouth dropped open as it hit the top right peak of the cross. She looked from Psyche to Theseus, disbelieving.

Theseus barked a laugh and applauded slowly and loudly.

'Does that count?' she asked quickly. Psyche shrugged.

'It's not the centre, but you hit the cross.'

'So I can come? To Taurus?' she asked Theseus.

'I guess so.' He smiled at her.

5

ERYX

Eryx was excited about seeing Taurus. As a child he had been told stories about the woodland realm, about the dryads that could transform themselves into trees, the elemental nymphs that were water one minute and wind the next, the numerous races of satyrs and their mystical lord Pan. He leaned over the railing eagerly as they soared past swirling orange clouds, approaching land. He ignored the ache in his chest.

'Dionysus is a tricky god,' said Antaeus behind him, and Eryx jumped at his voice.

'Captain,' he said, turning to him. 'How are you feeling?'

Antaeus grunted and Eryx instantly regretted asking. Busiris had confirmed that the giant was suffering from hypothermia when they got back to the *Orion*, and set about injecting warm salt water into his veins and covering him in heaps of blankets. Eryx had felt useless watching, waiting anxiously to see if Antaeus would regain consciousness. Busiris said that he must warm up slowly, or he would die anyway of shock, then disappeared into his rooms, refusing to talk about the Trial at all.

After a few hours, Antaeus did wake up. Eryx helped him swallow warm drink after warm drink and it wasn't long before he was able to move around. When Eryx had offered to help him bathe, Antaeus had growled at him, instructing him to forget that he had ever seen him in such a sorry state. The two brothers, Albion and Bergion, had had the sense to stay out of the way.

Now Antaeus leaned on the rail beside Eryx, dwarfing him, and Eryx bit back an urge to tell him he should probably put a shirt on to keep warm.

'You've never been to Taurus, have you?' Antaeus asked.

Eryx stole a glance at the snake tattoo, relieved to see the serpents writhing around on his back again. They had been completely still when his crew had removed his sodden clothes.

'No, Captain. I've always wanted to, though. I've heard they build their houses in the trees.'

Antaeus nodded. 'They do. There are three kingdoms in Taurus, each run by a different king, and they are constantly conniving and plotting to expand their own lands.' He snorted disdainfully. 'Not my sort of place.'

Eryx looked towards the dark patch of land, growing in the distance. 'Sounds like Busiris would fit in,' he said.

Antaeus laughed. 'Good choice of words, Brother. Only you and Busiris would *fit in* anywhere, literally. Most Taurus natives are small; their buildings will not accommodate giants.' He paused. 'Are you ready for another Trial?'

Eryx grinned before he could stop himself.

'I'm going with you?'

'You are, Eryx.'

6

LYSSA

Lyssa breathed out, long and slow, as she gratefully sank her head beneath the warm water. They had got Tenebrae's tank back to the cargo deck without incident, though the entire crew was giving it a wide berth. It had taken longer than she'd hoped it would to repair the hole that the Lady Lamia's ship had blasted in the hull, and her body ached from pushing herself emotionally and physically for what seemed like forever. How long ago had the Trials started? And now all four crews had one win apiece.

She brought her head up out of the water, pushing her wet hair away from her face, then reached for the soap. Inhaling the rose scent deeply, she couldn't help thinking of Phyleus. He'd bought the soap for the ship. He'd also lied about who he was. If he really was from Taurus, she should be talking to him right now. He might have information that could help them.

She knew why she was putting it off, though. She'd known he was more than the arrogant, whining boy she'd first seen standing behind Lady Lamia with a box of silver. He was fit and strong and smart and his self-belief went beyond aristocratic arrogance. He knew too much about Olympus, and while he moaned about the things they had done so far, she'd yet to see true fear in him.

The begrudging respect she was forming for him worried her. Whatever he would tell her now, learning who he had been before he joined the *Alastor* might shatter what she was starting to feel, ruin the trust she was building in him. She was worried that perhaps whatever he had to say would put a halt to the odd fluttery feeling in her stomach she was starting to get whenever his soft brown eyes met hers. She huffed and dunked her head back under the water, rubbing her hands through her hair to get the soap out. That fluttery feeling was annoyance, she chided herself.

'Lyssa?'

The voice in her head startled her so much she almost swallowed her bath-water. She sat up with a splash, choking. She'd never heard Phyleus's voice in her head before. The implications of that cut through her shock. The *Alastor* had accepted him.

'Captain! I've told you a hundred times it's *Captain*,' she snapped back.

'Even if nobody can hear us?'

'Especially if nobody can hear us.' There was a pause.

'Well, this is fun.' There was a hint of playfulness in his voice and even though Lyssa knew he couldn't see her she was suddenly very aware of her nakedness in the tub. 'I've never talked to somebody with my mind before.'

'Yeah, well, don't abuse it. What do you want?'

'We need to finish the conversation we started. The one where I tell you who I am.' She heard his tone change, not needing to see his facial expression to understand the seriousness.

'You really do have a high opinion of yourself. Why do

you think we'll care?' Lyssa stood up and stepped out of the copper tub, grabbing for a towel.

'Trust me, I wouldn't be telling you unless I had to. But I really do think you need to know. You and the rest of the crew.'

'Fine, fine.' She wrapped the towel around her hair and projected a message to the whole crew. 'Everybody, galley in fifteen minutes.'

'Thank you,' Phyleus said softly in her head.

THE GALLEY LOOKED SIGNIFICANTLY SMALLER with Nestor in it, Lyssa thought as they crowded around the long table.

'Thank you all for coming,' Phyleus said, wringing his hands and nodding at everybody. Lyssa groaned and brought her hands down flat on the table in front of her.

'Get on with it, Phyleus,' she said. He glared at her.

'Fine. I'm a prince.' He held her gaze as she felt her mouth fall open.

'You are joking,' she said as Len began to laugh beside her. Phyleus's cheeks flushed and he stood straight.

'It's true. I'm the second son of King Augeas of Taurus.'

Lyssa's heart hammered. Nobility was one thing, but royalty? She turned to the satyr.

'Len, you're from Taurus; wouldn't you know if we had a Taurean prince on board?' she demanded.

'Captain, I left Taurus thirty years ago and haven't been back. Phyleus hadn't even been born then.' Len looked Phyleus up and down appraisingly, still smiling. 'He does have the look of King Augeas, though,' he said.

Phyleus scowled. 'I hope I have nothing from my father.'

Lyssa recognised the vitriol in his face, in his words, and

she quirked an eyebrow. So Phyleus didn't like his father either?

'How does a prince end up as a slave on the Lady Lamia's ship?' asked Abderos.

'It's kind of a long story,' said Phyleus.

Lyssa stood up. She was struggling to work out how she felt. A prince? There were lots of princes in Olympus, to be fair, but it was a big thing to hide. Phyleus looked at her, no playfulness in his gaze.

'Captain, you must see why I didn't tell you. You gave me a hard enough time when you thought I was nobility. Would you have let me stay if I told you I was royalty?'

She knew immediately that the answer was no. She felt Epizon's eyes on her and she looked at the ceiling.

'No. No, I wouldn't have.' She found Phyleus's eyes. The fluttering in her belly was still there. 'Did you run away?'

He shook his head. 'I left with my family's blessing.'

'So you have no problem returning tomorrow?'

He scowled. 'No problem, no, but I had hoped not to return so soon after leaving.' His warm brown eyes were looking deep into hers, searching, and it was clear to her how much he wanted her approval. How much he wanted her to say that it was OK, that the tentative truce they were developing was still intact. Who was she to judge a person by their parents, their family or their upbringing? It made no difference where he came from. The man who had proved himself to her over the last four Trials was the one standing before her.

'Excellent. Maybe this will give us the edge we need to win this next Trial. Thank you for telling us, Phyleus,' she said. His face relaxed and Epizon stood up from the table.

'Drink, anybody?' he said and opened one of the wall cupboards.

'Does this mean we have to call you Your Highness?' said Abderos with a grin. Phyleus raised his eyebrows and put a thoughtful finger to his mouth.

'Now there's a thought...' he said.

'Don't even think about it. On the *Alastor*, you're still a deckhand,' Lyssa said as she took the glass of clear ouzo that Epizon offered her. Her first mate gave her a warm smile and his meaning was clear. Epizon approved of her reaction. She'd done the right thing. But the word *prince* kept churning around in her head.

7

EVADNE

Evadne was sitting on the wooden planks of the quarterdeck, her legs folded beneath her, staring into the gently flickering fire of the flame dish. She'd rather have been alone in her room, reading, but Hercules wanted her waiting for the next Trial announcement.

A book lay unopened by her side, all about the construction of Taurus's famous tree-houses but Evadne was too lost in thought to read. She'd known who Hercules was when she joined the crew of the *Hybris*. She'd thought that she would be able to keep him on her side, to use her charm to ensure she got what she wanted. It had been foolish of her to never properly consider what Hercules had the potential to do. What would he could do *to her*.

The fire crackled loudly, pulling her from her reverie.

'Captain, the flame dish,' she projected mentally to Hercules. The flames in front of her turned white and leaped high in the dish, a foot tall, before an image appeared. It was the blond Trial-announcer, his now familiar face beaming, his perky voice triggering both irritation and apprehension.

'Good day, Olympus! So our heroes have almost reached Taurus but they've yet to find out what awaits them when they get there.' He gave an exaggerated wink and Evadne pulled a face. She heard boots on the deck behind her and glanced at Hercules as he came to a stop by her side, Asterion just behind him. 'Dionysus will meet the heroes and one member of their crew at the Palace of Elis, where they will find out what they need to do to win the fifth Trial and take the lead. Good luck, heroes!' The image faded from the flames as they shrank down to their normal size and flickered orange again. Hercules snorted.

'That tells us nothing we didn't already know,' he huffed.

Evadne said nothing. Elis was the largest kingdom in Taurus. She'd visited once before, with her family. She'd seen the palace from the outside and had longed to see what it was like on the inside but her parents, wealthy as they were, hadn't warranted an invitation from royalty. The spark of adventure kindled in her gut.

'Who will you be taking with you, Captain?' Evadne asked tentatively.

Hercules considered her a moment. 'Do you wish for a chance to redeem yourself?' he said eventually.

She looked meekly at the floor. 'I do, Captain.'

'Good. Then you shall have it.'

EVADNE'S EYES sparkled as the *Hybris* sailed to a stop by a long wooden branch of the enormous tree that housed the Palace of Elis. They'd flown over dense forest, streams sparkling through the lush greenery, until they had reached a copse of the largest trees she had ever seen. There were nine of them in total and this one, in the centre, was at least a hundred feet taller than its neighbours. Wooden structures filled the gaps between branches as wide as the *Hybris*, brightly painted and covered in tiny glowing lights. The network of homes was connected by rope ladders and wooden bridges covered in hanging lanterns. She squinted at the buildings as they passed, trying to find evidence of how they had been built, but she couldn't see a single join. It was as though they had been carved from the trees themselves.

The branch currently acting as a pier for the ships in the Trials was broad enough to accommodate ten people across its width, and ran all the way up to beautiful arched wooden doors set into the trunk of the central tree. Rising from the wood above were more seamless structures, weaving in and out of the trunk and its branches. They stood out from the lower buildings not only for their size, but for their shining patterns painted everywhere. Dancing golden lights made the patterns look like they were moving in the shadow of the trees' foliage.

The *Alastor* and the *Virtus* were already docked on the other side of the branch. Evadne wondered for a moment about the *Orion* until a shadow fell over their own sails, and the giants' *Zephyr* came overhead and descended in front of them, drawing level with the flat branch. Hercules vaulted over the railings and onto the branch without a sideways look at her. She hopped lightly up onto the railings after him, adjusting her belt as she landed on the wood of the tree. Captain Lyssa and the brown-haired boy Evadne remembered was called Phyleus did the same on the other side of the branch.

Theseus and the beautiful Hedone were already standing there, waiting. Evadne watched as Hedone's eyes fell on Hercules and stayed there. There was a thud as Antaeus joined them on the branch and she suppressed a small smile at the sight of Eryx next to him, five feet shorter with his dark hair tied up in a knot. She was glad his chest had healed. And surprised by the fact that she was glad. A shimmering light in front of the double doors caught everybody's attention and they all turned as Dionysus appeared. He seemed to grow in front of them until it was easy to see him clearly. He was wearing leather fighting trousers, no shirt and a beaming grin. His hair flopped over his forehead as he threw both hands in the air and bellowed, 'Heroes!'

Evadne couldn't help the smile that crossed her face.

'I'm so glad you're here!' Dionysus walked towards them, his ruddy face crinkling in a genuine smile. He didn't look like the other gods, Evadne thought. 'Come, come, we must feast before we begin this Trial. It is very important to enjoy the finer things in life,' he said with a wink. 'But I see none of you are dressed for an occasion. We can fix that,' he said to himself, nodding. 'Yes, yes we can definitely fix that.'

Evadne took a sharp breath as she felt movement against her body and looked down. Her fighting leathers were gone and in their place was a tight-fitting red floor-length gown. She took a step backwards, putting her hands to her bodice as she did so. The dress was low-cut and pushed her breasts up so that they looked bigger than they really were. It was cinched at the waist with a long ribbon, making the material flow out over her hips and giving her a shapely look that her lithe, athletic form didn't usually have.

She looked around at the others. Captain Lyssa looked the most different. The headscarf was gone from her flowing red curls and they fell around her shoulders, drawing attention to the one-sleeved gold satin toga clinging to her body. Deep gold brocade lined the edges and the expensive-looking material flattered her beautifully. Evadne almost laughed at the look on Lyssa's face, though, as she surveyed the dress, picking up the folds of fabric and dropping them again in confusion and frustration. Phyleus said something to her and she punched him in the arm, making him stumble back laughing.

A pang of jealousy took Evadne by complete surprise, and she turned to Hercules. He looked resplendent in a traditional black toga, revealing half of his fine chest, and a fine circlet of gold topped his dark hair. His gaze was nowhere near her, though. It was fixed on Hedone.

She was now dressed in a gossamer silk gown that wrapped tightly around her chest and was held up by ribbons that came around her neck and crisscrossed all the way down her back to the low-slung skirt of the dress. Jealousy fully took hold of Evadne and she screwed her face up. Was she jealous of the way Hercules was looking at Hedone? Or was she just jealous of Hedone's beauty?

'Come,' boomed Dionysus. We must feast with our hosts.' He turned, and the carved doors swung open.

Dionysus wanted to travel from Ikaria to Naxos so he hired a ship of pirates to take him. But they took him captive to sell on as a slave in Asia. In response, he turned the mast and the oars of the boat into snakes and covered the whole boat in ivy and filled it with the sound of flutes playing. The pirates all went mad and jumped into the ocean, where they were turned into dolphins.

EXCERPT FROM

The Library by Apollodorus

Written 300–100 BC

Paraphrased by Eliza Raine

8

LYSSA

Lyssa shifted uncomfortably in the heavy satin dress, fiddling with the skirt as she tried to pay attention to what King Augeas was saying. She was all too aware of Phyleus's eyes drifting to her bare shoulder, and it was making her cheeks flush.

They were seated at a dining table ten times the size of the one in the galley on the *Alastor*, in a room carved from a hollow of the giant tree itself. Antaeus, the giant, hadn't been able to fit through the carved doors and had looked horrified when Dionysus had waved his hand and shrunk him by five feet. Although Eryx hadn't needed shrinking, he had looked equally as uncomfortable as she was about being dressed in a formal toga and she certainly wouldn't want to get on the wrong side of either him or Antaeus now.

The dining hall was lit by what must have been a hundred dancing fairy lights, suspended in mid-air and casting a warm flickering glow over everybody in the room. The lighting, the clothes: they were clearly meant to flatter everybody. Dionysus sat in the centre of his side of the table, still bare-chested, laughing uproariously at everything that was said to him. The royal family of Elis sat either side of him, King Augeas and his eldest son on his right and the King's wife and daughter on his left.

Phyleus and his father had so far only traded polite nods but Lyssa hadn't failed to notice the glares the King kept throwing his estranged son. They were sitting at the far end of their side of the table, Theseus and Hedone next to them, then Hercules and Evadne and lastly Antaeus and Eryx.

A feast rivalling that of the starting ceremony had been laid out before them; olives, meats and fruits, including even strawberries. Lyssa had loaded her plate with the tiny red fruits and had a steaming mug of hot black coffee in front of her.

'Are you going to eat anything other than strawberries?' asked Phyleus. Lyssa shrugged. 'It's just, they're not very nutritious, are they?' he said.

She snorted at his pile of whitish flatbreads.

'And those are?'

'Probably not,' he conceded. He tore off a chunk and used it to scoop up a thick red paste. 'But I missed this,' he said.

'Why did you leave?' Lyssa asked before she could stop herself.

His face darkened. 'I'm the second son. That means my father has little use for me. He sent me... He sent me to do something that most people would not survive.'

Lyssa stopped eating and looked at him. 'Why?'

'Because on the off-chance I did survive, I might come back with something he needed.'

Lyssa's eyebrows drew together. 'And did you?' she asked.

Phyleus looked at his father, deep in conversation with his older brother.

'Yes,' he said quietly. 'But he doesn't need to know that.'

'Huh.' Lyssa turned back to her plate of strawberries. 'Maybe we have more in common than I first thought,' she said without looking at him.

'I did tell you that, some time ago,' Phyleus said.

'Yeah, well. I don't know if you've noticed, but...' She met his eyes, warm and honest and open. '... sometimes I can be a little stubborn,' she said quietly. A smile that lit up his eyes took over Phyleus's face and she couldn't help but give a small one in return.

'Phyleus.' They both turned to the source of the voice. It was Phyleus's mother. She was a delicate-looking woman, with slight, high cheekbones and a well-defined jawline. Her eyes and hair were the same warm brown as Phyleus's. 'How have you been?'

Phyleus shrugged.

'Well, I was kidnapped by a slaver, caught as a stowaway on a smugglers' ship and have recently been fighting for my life, and immortality, in the Trials. So pretty busy, really.' He tore another lump off his bread. For once, Lyssa admired his arrogance. He was acting like for all the world he didn't care that he was back in the place he had deliberately left. But the way he had just spoken about his father... Lyssa wasn't so sure.

AT THE TINGING sound of metal against glass, everybody looked towards Dionysus, who got to his feet holding a glass of red wine.

'I would like to propose a toast,' he said. He waved his hand and identical glasses appeared in front of each of the captains. Phyleus looked sharply at Lyssa as she picked hers up. She frowned at him. 'Captains, raise your glass.' Lyssa did so, wondering why she could see slight panic in Phyleus eyes. 'You have taken on a grave responsibility for the ultimate prize. You are heroes. To the heroes!' Dionysus said, lifting his glass high in the air, then swigging deeply from it.

'To the heroes,' chanted everybody else in the room.

'Wait—' Phyleus started to say as Lyssa tipped the wine into her mouth. Exasperation crossed his face for a second, then he grabbed her face in his hands and kissed her.

He did it so fast Lyssa didn't know how to react. She was stunned. Wine sloshed from her mouth to his and she felt his tongue against her lips. Energy fizzed across her skin, her body reacting without her permission. Her brain kicked in, though, and she pulled back from him.

'What the hell are you doing?' she hissed.

'I'm sorry, I really, really am sorry.' He looked it, too. Dionysus clapped slowly and Lyssa's eyes snapped to him.

'Nice try, young Phyleus, but she must drink it all.'

Phyleus looked at her glass, still half full of red wine, then back at Lyssa. 'The wine,' he said resignedly. 'It induces madness.'

Panic and outrage erupted around the room and Dionysus held up a hand to silence them all.

'He's right. God of wine and madness, remember?' Dionysus pointed at himself with a massive grin. 'You have about fifteen minutes until the effects kick in. Captain Lyssa, if you please?' He gestured at what remained of her drink.

Madness? Why would she drink something that would make her mad? Her hand moved towards the glass of its own volition and she started.

'Don't make this difficult for yourself,' the wine god chided. She seethed, knowing it was pointless to resist, but still refusing to yield.

'Lyssa,' whispered Phyleus. She barked a cry of anger and picked up the glass, throwing the wine into her mouth.

It tasted so divine that for a moment she resented Phyleus for stealing half of it away from her. As she swallowed and the taste faded, though, the implications of what he had done sank in. She'd swallowed none of that first mouthful. He had taken it all. She would have had half of what the other captains drank. That could be all she needed to beat them.

For his fifth labour Hercules was asked by King Augeas of Elis to remove all the dung from his stable of cattle in just a day. Hercules agreed with him that if he succeeded he could have the tithe of the cattle. Augeas's son, Phyleus, bore witness as Hercules diverted two rivers through the stables, cleaning them completely. Augeas refused to pay and Phyleus was called to confirm what Hercules had done. Augeas exiled both his son and Hercules from Elis.

EXCERPT FROM

The Library by Apollodorus

Written 300–100 BC

Paraphrased by Eliza Raine

9

ERYX

Eryx looked from the empty wine glass in Antaeus's hand to his furious face.

'Madness?' the giant growled through his teeth. 'If this is true, Eryx, I will need you to help me.'

Eryx nodded, silently. He prayed that by the time they got to whatever they had to do, Antaeus would be returned to his normal size again.

'Excellent,' said Dionysus, and clapped his hands together. 'Now that we have all had our fill of refreshments, let's get on with the Trial!' He gestured to the king. 'Good King Augeas here keeps many exotic creatures in his palace stables. And by exotic, I do of course mean the bloodthirsty killer type. Each of you will get a stall in the stables to clear out. A cord at the back of the stall will flood the animals' pens with water; all you have to do is pull it. But it must be the captain who pulls it. Oh, and then get back up through the palace to the throne room. First one back wins.' He beamed at everybody in the room as he drew his hands to his mouth. 'And as a little bonus, you'll also win the loyalty of whatever creature you were mucking out. Don't say I don't care about you lovely folk!' He grinned, wagging his finger at them all.

Eryx stared, trying to make sense of what he was saying. They had to muck out animals?

'To the stables!' Dionysus sang happily, and everything went black.

WHEN HE OPENED his eyes a second later, Eryx was standing in line with the others, facing a closed stable door. Antaeus was beside him, blinking in confusion but mercifully back to his full height.

Eryx turned slowly on the spot. There was a wall behind them, but when he looked up there was no ceiling, just a thick canopy of trees shading them. The line of stable doors seemed to stretch forever in both directions and he saw the others looking around nervously too, each in front of a different door. How did they get out once they had pulled the cord?

'On my mark, good heroes,' came Dionysus's voice. Eryx tensed, facing the stall again. 'Captain Lyssa: you, my dear, will be facing...' The god paused overly long and the girl snorted with impatience. '... a chimera! Good luck with that!' he boomed. 'Captain Hercules, you lucky thing, you have a manticore! Clever Captain Theseus gets a clever monster, a sphinx! And lastly, but oh so not leastly, Captain Antaeus gets my favourite, a panther! Go!' he bellowed, and the stable doors swung open.

10

LYSSA

'Phyleus, did he say chimera?' said Lyssa, uncharacteristically nervous.

'Yes,' Phyleus answered, looking left towards all the other heroes, who were cautiously approaching the stalls.

'It was a chimera that took Ab's legs,' she said quietly. He looked at her, sympathy and warmth filling his expression. 'Thanks for taking half the wine,' she murmured. 'But wouldn't it have been better to have one of us sane?'

Phyleus shook his head. 'The royal families on Taurus give the wine to their children, so they develop an immunity to it.' Lyssa looked horrified.

'You send your children mad?'

'Nobody believes a drink is poisoned if you are also drinking it. They've been doing it for centuries.'

This time Lyssa's face filled with sympathy. 'They did that to you?'

Phyleus sighed and took her hand.

'Come on, we need to get going, before the madness kicks in,' he said, and tugged her towards the stall.

Lyssa thought it might already be too late. There was a short passage in front of them, with rakes and shovels propped against one wall and she was sure they were whispering to her. She gripped Phyleus's hand tighter, and he glanced at her.

'Can you fight a chimera?' he asked her.

She laughed, surprised by the sound. 'Why would I want to fight a chimera?'

'Well, you won't have to if we can get past it and pull the cord. But just in case... Are you ready to fight?'

Lyssa thought about the question as they reached the second stable door. There was no roof above them, she realised, and she tipped her head back to look at the huge green leaves overhead. Was she ready to fight? No. She didn't want to fight. She wanted to fly.

'I want to fly,' she told Phyleus.

'Shit,' he said. She frowned at him.

'Will you fly with me?' she asked. Vines were growing from behind his ears, curling up and over his thick hair and intertwining to make a crown. 'I'd like to fly with a prince.' She smiled.

A loud, angry snort pulled her attention back to the door. 'What's in there?' she asked.

Phyleus blew out a long breath. 'Lyssa, listen to me. I need you to get angry. Call your power.'

Something was scratching at the stable door and she reached out.

'No!' said Phyleus but she ignored him, pulling on the rope handle. It wasn't fair to keep animals cooped up.

LYSSA SCREAMED as the door swung open. A lion stood before her, spreading its huge red leathery wings and flicking its scaled dragon's tail. *Not a lion*, she thought, and that word rang through her head again: *chimera*. Chimeras had three heads. The goat head looked harmless enough, its dull ivory horns curled in and unable to do much damage. But the dragon head... As red as the massive wings and horribly reminiscent of the Hydra with its jutting horns, it opened its mouth, showing glowing embers deep inside its throat. There was a metallic thud next to her and she looked down, surprised to find she was sitting on the dusty ground, a shovel tumbling to a stop beside her.

'Pick it up!' yelled Phyleus.

A chimera took Abderos's legs. The thought stilled her hand. She couldn't fight a chimera. They took people's legs. Heart-stopping fear gripped her chest and she looked desperately at her own legs, pulling at the golden gown. They weren't there. Bile rose in her throat as she scrabbled frantically at the fabric. She had no legs!

Tears spilled from her eyes as she screamed, drowning out the sound of the lion's roar.

11

HERCULES

'Have you seen a manticore before, Captain?' asked Evadne nervously as they approached the inner stable door. The wooden surface of the door seemed to ripple, and Hercules shook his head, trying to clear his wobbly vision.

'Where's my lion skin?' he asked her, ignoring her question.

'Dionysus changed our clothes. I don't know,' she said. He looked at her, startled by her blood-red dress. Concern was clear on her face.

'Captain, do you remember what you have to do when you get in there?' she said slowly.

He snarled. Of course he did. He had to... kill the beast.

'Kill the manticore,' he barked, and laid his hand on the rope handle of the door.

'No! You need to pull the cord at the back of the stall.'

He took a long breath, the floor tilting beneath him. 'Which will be easy, once we have killed the beast,' he growled, and pulled the door open.

The manticore sprang at him before he had time to

register its presence. He dropped to the ground but he wasn't fast enough rolling away and the creature's claw sliced through the skin of his shoulder. Pounding energy flooded his body and he leaped to his feet, swinging his arm in a punch as the thing sprang for him again. His fist connected and the manticore yelped as it flew backwards and bounced off the stable wall.

Hercules squinted, trying to focus his swimming vision. The manticore looked like a horned lion, save for the lethal scorpion tail curled up over its back. The stinger was glowing red.

'If the stinger touches you, you'll die,' he heard Evadne say. He glanced at her. Red. She was covered in red. It was a dress, he told himself, but images flashed before him. Another woman, with red hair, covered in red. Not a dress, but blood. And suddenly he was there again, strength unrivalled by anything he had ever felt burning through his body as he dropped the poker on the floor and stared down at Megara. His wife.

He was invincible. He had the power to take life. How had he never known what this could feel like? A wave of revulsion crashed over the elation. His wife... The blood... What had he done? He took a halting step forward and then remembered. She was going to leave him. She was going to take their children and leave him. This wasn't his fault. He heard a sob and looked up. A flash of red hair disappeared from the parlour doorway. His daughter. As he took a step towards the door, convulsions ripped through his body. He roared as he dropped to his hands and knees, forcing his eyes shut against the pain.

'All power has a cost, Hercules,' said Hera's voice in his mind. 'And you will pay the price.'

Forcing his eyes open again, he recoiled when he

realised he was kneeling in Megara's blood. He held his hands up in front of him, and watched the red liquid drip down his skin.

His control over his anger, so carefully balanced on a knife edge for so long, broke completely.

12

EVADNE

Evadne cowered in the doorway as Hercules roared so loudly that the manticore froze. He had started screaming and convulsing and the beast had been confused enough to stay back, stalking slowly around its thrashing prey, until the man had suddenly launched himself to his feet and made that awful inhuman sound.

The look on his face was nothing short of terrifying. His eyes were wild, filled with fire and hatred, and her mouth fell open in fear. The manticore hissed and leaped for him but he kicked out, catching it squarely in the chest. The scorpion tail flicked around as it spun away on the ground but Hercules ducked and reached for the beast's back leg. He dragged the manticore back to him, easily dodging the shining stinger, a disturbing laugh bubbling out of his mouth.

Evadne sank to the floor, gripping the lintel, nausea rolling through her at the twisted look on his face. Hercules had scared her before, but she had never seen him like this. The manticore snarled and snapped as one of Hercules's huge arms wrapped around its middle and the other gripped its tail. The snarl turned to a roar as he began to twist his hand, the tail bending at an unnatural angle. Evadne wanted to look away but she couldn't. Hercules's laugh got louder as he twisted further, the manticore's roars morphing into howls.

'Stop,' Evadne whispered, tears beginning to roll down her cheeks as her stomach roiled. A sickening crack accompanied a screech of pain and the manticore thrashed in Hercules's iron grip. But he didn't stop. He pulled, and Evadne forced her eyes closed. Why wouldn't he just kill it? Why was he torturing it? She'd been wrong. She'd been so, so wrong to believe that he wasn't dangerous.

Something wet and hot sprayed her and she kept her eyes squeezed shut as she retched, knowing it was the creature's blood.

The howls and screeches stopped and Hercules's maniacal laugh died to a frightening chuckle. Evadne opened her eyes, forcing herself to survey the stall. Hercules was covered in blood and gore, rocking on his heels, his eyes unfocused and vacant. Around him lay the manticore, in several pieces. He had ripped the creature apart.

She turned away, horror overwhelming her as she retched again.

13

HEDONE

Hedone tried to steady her shaking hands as she picked up the shovel from against the pen wall.

'Hedone?' Theseus said her name as a question.

'Yes, Captain?'

'I... I can't see very well. You're going to have to open this door.' He came to a stumbling halt in front of her as he said it.

'What's wrong? Why can't you see?' She hurried to his side. His dark skin was pale, his eyes unfocused.

'There are stars. Stars everywhere. They're blocking everything out.' He reached a hand towards her with a marvelling expression. 'You're so... so...' he trailed off, staring at her chest.

'Theseus, you need to get it together,' she said, grabbing his cheek and giving his head a small shake. 'I can't face a sphinx alone. What is a sphinx anyway?'

As she hoped it would, the question refocused him. His gaze moved to her eyes and he pushed his braids back from his face and blinked fast.

'It's like a lion, but it has wings and a woman's face.' Hedone frowned. 'It eats people.' Hedone stiffened. 'And asks riddles.'

'Riddles?' she repeated.

He nodded.

'That's why you got the sphinx,' she realised. 'Clever Theseus, and all that.'

'I am clever,' he said indignantly, then tipped his head back. 'So's she,' he said, pointing up to the leafy canopy above them.

'Who?' Hedone followed his pointing finger.

'Her. Look at her tail! It's beautiful.'

Hedone could see nothing. She blew out a long breath, gripped the shovel and pulled on the rope door-handle.

THE SPHINX WAS SITTING on her haunches in the middle of the stall, her wings spread wide and her stunning face serene and calm. She didn't blink her orange eyes as Hedone and Theseus stepped into the stall, but spoke in a deep, soothing voice.

'What has an eye but cannot see?'

Theseus barked a laugh and clawed at the air in front of him.

'I have fifty eyes,' he murmured, 'but all I can see is birds...' His voice was filled with wonder and he waved his arms in front of him again, as though trying to catch something. Hedone grabbed him as he stumbled forward, her heart missing a beat as the sphinx flicked her eyes towards him.

'Incorrect,' she said. 'You may try twice more.'

'What happens if we get it wrong?' asked Hedone, her voice coming out as little more than a whisper.

The sphinx's wings quivered as she said, 'You die.'

A PIERCING SCREAM filled the stables and Hedone and Theseus's heads snapped towards the sound. It turned into a long, loud moan and Hedone's skin began to crawl. Was that Hercules? It was definitely a man. She hated herself for the thought that immediately filled her mind: *Please let it be one of the giants.* The howls began to die down, then a roar filled her ears, so full of anger and pain that her knees went weak. It *was* Hercules. She needed to help him.

Her heart pounding, she turned back to Theseus, snapping her fingers in front of his face.

'Do you know the answer? Theseus? What has an eye but cannot see?'

He looked at her vaguely. 'Eyes everywhere. But they can all see.'

Exasperation filled her and she tried to block out the animalistic howls coming from the other stall. Theseus gripped her arm hard, making her cry out. 'Needles!' he exclaimed urgently, then his face relaxed again and he looked up, entranced by something only he could see.

Needles. He was right. A needle had an eye but could not see.

'A needle,' Hedone said to the sphinx. She bowed her head.

'Correct. I'm tall when I'm young and short when I'm old. What am I?'

Another howl ripped through the air and tears filled her eyes.

'Not another one,' she moaned. The sphinx's face didn't move. 'Theseus? Did you hear that?'

Theseus looked at her. 'Eyes everywhere,' he murmured

again and reached out to touch her face. She pulled back and the vacant expression on his face changed. Panic filled his eyes and he wrenched his arm out of her grip. 'They're coming,' he whispered, looking over her shoulder. Hedone spun around in alarm but there was nothing behind her, only the featureless stable wall.

'There's nothing coming, Theseus,' she said, as calmly as she could manage. He shook his head hard, his braids swinging, then sank to the floor, covering his face with his hands.

'No, no, no, Theseus, I need you!' Hedone dropped into a crouch beside him and tried to pull his hands down, but he cried out and turned away from her. What was she going to do? She could hear nothing from the other stall now. Was that good or bad? What if Hercules had been injured or worse? She stood up, trying to swallow her rising panic. She would just have to get past the sphinx herself. What was tall when it was young and short when it was old? She took a deep breath, sorting through her whirling thoughts. What got shorter over time? Nothing living, she thought. All living things grew. So it had to be something you use up. The sphinx had said tall and short, so it was something that lost height. The answer hit her in a rush and she blurted it out before she could stop herself.

'A candle!'

The sphinx nodded her head again.

'Correct. The last riddle. What is as light as a feather but cannot be held by the world's strongest man for more than a few minutes?'

Dismay rolled over Hedone. *Another* one? She glanced down at Theseus, who had drawn his knees up and was rocking backwards and forwards, his face still covered.

She would just have to work this one out by herself too.

14

ERYX

ntaeus was panting in the corner of the reeking stall, crouched low to the ground, wild eyes darting around the small room. In the opposite corner a huge sleek black cat paced back and forth, guarding a long pull cord. Eryx wanted desperately to try to get to it himself but Dionysus had said that only the captains could pull the rope and flood the stall. Instead, he darted out from the doorway again, waving a rake at the lethally fanged creature. It paused for a second, flicking its tail and giving a languid hiss, then resumed its pacing.

Eryx had been repeatedly trying to distract the panther to no avail. It was smart. It knew Antaeus was trying to get past and it wasn't going to move. Antaeus shouted from his corner and frustration welled in Eryx. He was impotent to help, both with the panther and with whatever his captain was seeing that he couldn't. He hated it. He hated not being able to do anything. He skipped backwards, not taking his eyes off the cat, until he reached his captain. He hooked his arm under Antaeus's and pulled him awkwardly to his feet.

'Come on, Captain. Let's try again,' he said lightly.

Antaeus bared his teeth. 'They're everywhere,' he hissed.

'Well, let's concentrate on this one for now,' Eryx said, pointing his rake at the panther. 'If you pull that cord, they'll all go away.' Eryx had no idea what Antaeus thought was everywhere, or if they would go away if he pulled the cord, but he didn't know what else to say. Antaeus gripped his arm.

'The cord,' he repeated.

'Exactly, Captain. The cord. Just don't let the cat get you.'

'Cat?' Panic filled Antaeus's voice.

'Yes. That cat,' Eryx pointed again at the panther. Antaeus looked along the rake and growled when his eyes settled on the big cat. It looked straight back at him, tail swishing, its gleaming yellow eyes unblinking, challenging. 'I'll go—' Eryx started to speak but Antaeus ripped his arm free and launched himself at the cord. The panther jumped at the same time and they collided mid-air, crashing to the ground in a flurry of claws and snarls. Eryx swore and threw himself into the fight.

Something hard hit Lyssa and she tumbled sideways. Everything around her was hot and her face was near something that smelled bad.

'Lyssa, listen to me!' The voice was too loud and she didn't have time to listen. She needed to find her legs.

All of a sudden she was hauled upright and the shock stilled her mad scrabbling. She looked down at herself, panting, and lifted her golden skirts. She could see her leather boots. And in them, her ankles. Relief flooded her and she laughed out loud.

'My legs!' She looked around happily for somebody to tell and stepped back in surprise at what she saw. Half the stall she was standing in was on fire, and a three-headed monster was pawing the ground through the flames, red wings beating slowly.

'What...?'

'Lyssa.' Phyleus appeared in front of her. A wave of clarity washed over her as she looked into his eyes. 'Lyssa, you have to pull that cord. Behind the chimera. Do you see it?' He was gripping her shoulders. She looked past him, past the lion head baring its massive teeth, past the flickering flames. She nodded.

'I see it,' she whispered.

'Concentrate on that and nothing else,' he said clearly. She nodded again. 'Go,' he said and released her, running towards the side of the stall that wasn't crackling with fire.

As soon as his hands left her body her vision swam again, as if he had removed her anchor to reality. She swallowed the sick feeling rising in her and focused on the rope hanging down in the far corner of the room. *Concentrate.*

'Come and get me!' Phyleus bellowed suddenly and all three of the chimera's heads swung towards him. Lyssa didn't wait to think through what she was doing. She ran. The ground shifted and tilted under her feet and for a brief second everything around her seemed to be covered in vines. Even the chimera was covered, its beautiful red wings wrapped in the dark green plants. She slowed and heard Phyleus yell, 'Concentrate!'

She fixed her eyes on the cord again and the vines receded. Red and orange light filled her vision and she realised hazily that it had come from the chimera. From the dragon head. Fire. It was fire. The beast wasn't going to move towards Phyleus, it was going to try to burn him from where it was standing, guarding the rope. She felt her power fizzing under her skin and she flexed her fists, pulling on the familiar feeling. As the Rage built she felt it course through her body, forcing out the haziness, sharpening the world around her.

The goat head saw her first and bleated loudly, causing the

other two to snap towards her. She dropped into a skid, pulling her satin skirts up and lying almost flat along the ground as she threw her power into the movement. She moved fast, wincing as the dragon head ducked down towards her. It missed by inches and she sailed straight under the belly of the great creature. It jumped and stamped as she spun out on the other side and tripped over the dress as she scrambled to her feet.

The creature's massive scaled tail smashed into her stomach as it turned and she was knocked high into the air. It was as though she was falling in slow motion. The stall was burning and she could see Phyleus through the flames, yelling and pointing behind her. She threw her arms out to her sides, feeling like she was moving through mud.

Something scratched against her wrist, then her back hit the wall hard and she bounced off it, landing on her back-side. The chimera's lion head roared as the dragon head reared back, orange embers filling its open maw. This was it.

'It's right next to you!' Phyleus screamed. She turned her head. The rope cord was swinging gently next to her. She blinked and pulled it.

The back panel of the stall, to her left, began lifting with a loud clanking sound. The chimera swung all three of its heads that way and pawed the ground excitedly, then bounded towards the widening opening. As soon as the wall had lifted far enough it ducked down and squeezed under, disappearing into the foliage beyond.

Lyssa let out a long breath and Phyleus ran to her, jumping over the burning lumps of hay. He grabbed both of her hands and pulled but she stayed where she was, leaning against the wall.

'I need to rest,' she told him. And she did. She was so, so tired.

'We can't yet. We need to get back to the throne room. Then you can rest.' He pulled again and she sighed. The ground beneath her was wet and she looked down. Water was rushing into the room from the forest.

'Do you promise?' she asked Phyleus.

He stopped pulling and crouched down beside her. He put his hand out and gently pushed away the loose curls that had been sticking to her face.

'I promise.' She watched his lips move as he said it. They were nice lips. 'Lyssa, we need to go, now.' She took his hand and let him pull her to her feet.

Together they followed the chimera out into the forest.

16

HEDONE

Theseus leaped up suddenly, startling Hedone out of her thoughts.

'They're here!' he hissed, spinning and ducking, his eyes wild.

'Theseus, there's nothing here, it's OK,' she told him. He ignored her, throwing his hands over his head. Hedone stepped towards him and gripped his arms gently. 'Theseus, look at me.'

She tried to get him to fix his wild gaze on her but his eyes darted around the small room and he pulled away from her, stumbling. Hedone's breath caught as he flailed his arms and lurched towards the sphinx. She tried to grab for him again but he side-stepped, covering his face with his hands once more and brushing his booted foot against the sphinx's outstretched paw. The creature reacted in a heart-beat. She was up on all fours, her huge wings filling the small room as her serene eyes flashed with fire.

'Touch me again and you will both die,' she said, her voice loud enough to make Theseus stop staggering long enough for Hedone to pull him to her. 'Now, answer the riddle. What is as light as a feather but cannot be held by the world's strongest man for more than a few minutes?'

'Theseus, did you hear that?' Hedone shook him desperately. Try as she might, she couldn't work out what the answer was. She knew it wasn't a physical object, as the world's strongest man would be able to hold anything that was as light as a feather, but she didn't know what it could be.

'Responsibility?' she said, screwing up her face as she said it. She knew it was wrong.

'Incorrect. You have one try remaining.' The sphinx's wing rippled.

'Theseus, please, look at me,' Hedone took his jaw in her hand and held his face steady in front of her own.

'You're beautiful,' he whispered as he focused on her.

'What is the answer to the riddle?' she asked him, through gritted teeth. He stared back at her vacantly. 'What can nobody hold for more than a few minutes?' she half shouted at him.

'Unless you live under the sea, your breath.' He shrugged and took a huge gulp of air and held it, his cheeks puffing out.

Hedone stared at him a moment. He was right. She spun around to face the sphinx.

'Your breath,' she said.

'Correct,' said the sphinx and stepped to one side, sitting back down on her haunches. The cord hung from the far corner of the room and Hedone jumped as Theseus suddenly gasped for air behind her.

'I held my breath,' he said.

'I know, Theseus, well done,' she muttered as she grabbed his elbow and pulled him past the sphinx to the rope.

17

LYSSA

'How are you feeling?' Phyleus asked Lyssa as they pulled themselves up yet another rope ladder.

'Thirsty. And a little dizzy,' she answered.

'Still seeing vines everywhere?'

'There *are* vines everywhere,' she scowled. Phyleus laughed.

'Good point,' he said. They'd been climbing up the trunk of the gargantuan tree that housed the palace for what seemed like forever, and Lyssa wanted to cause Dionysus permanent damage for making her do it in a dress. At least she still had her boots on. She wouldn't have made it more than ten feet off the ground in heels.

'Will the others still be mad from the wine?' she asked Phyleus as he held a hand down to her and pulled her off the rope ladder and onto a wide branch supporting a small wooden hut.

'Yeah,' he said, walking towards the next ladder. 'Yeah, a glass that size will last a while.'

She shuddered. 'It was horrible. I thought... I thought I

had no legs.' Her heart ached for Abderos, for what he must have gone through.

'The others will get it worse.'

Lyssa waited for him to get halfway up the ladder, then stepped onto it herself.

'And you had to drink a lot of it?' she asked him.

'It's different when you're a kid,' Phyleus answered. 'No inner demons to face. Just scary monsters.' Lyssa wondered again what his father had made him do that should have killed him.

'And your brother and sister had to drink it too?'

'Yep. Until they were immune. The door's here.' She climbed up onto the branch and instead of another rope ladder, there was door into the trunk of the tree.

'Is that the throne room?'

Phyleus shook his head. 'No. There's a staircase to the throne room. But it's not a normal staircase,' he warned her. She raised an eyebrow. 'It'll make you think you're mad again. Just make sure that you follow me, and keep moving up. Never go down.'

'Never go down,' she repeated.

He smiled.

'We're nearly there, Captain,' he said.

THE SECOND they stepped through the carved door the world tilted again. They were in a square stairwell with a black-and-white chequered floor and stairs spiralling up around the four walls, but the checks seemed to move and shift before her eyes.

'Ignore the floor, keep moving up,' Phyleus said and started up the stairs. She followed him and gasped as her boots made contact with the first step. The floor was *actually* tilting. She pushed both hands against the wall as the room swung to the side, slowly rotating. She was turning upside down, she realised.

'What's—' she started to say to Phyleus, but he was gone. 'Phyleus?' she called loudly. 'Where are you?' There was no answer. Black-and-white steps just spiralled endlessly and emptily ahead of her. The room came slowly to a halt and she hesitantly let go of the wall. She touched her hair, which was no longer falling over her shoulders but hanging from her head towards what had been the ceiling and now seemed to be the floor. Keep moving up, Phyleus had said. Which way was up?

She was now at the top. She took a step backwards, and the floor lurched again, a section of the staircase swinging out this time, the square room widening to accommodate it. She stared as new steps grew, zigzagging higher. She walked quickly towards them, closing her eyes when the lurching motion made her feel sick.

THE STAIRCASE MOVED, growing, shrinking and rotating repeatedly, but Lyssa did exactly what Phyleus had told her to do and kept going up, even when it meant retracing her steps. The longer she was in the black-and-white room, the more surreal it felt and the less sure she was that she would ever get out. The feeling of being trapped hovered at the edge of her awareness but she refused to entertain it. She knew that as soon as she let it in the thought would cripple her, panic turning to useless Rage. *Phyleus told you what to do, just keep going up*, she told herself calmly over and over again. But the steps were endless and the feeling was growing. She was never going to get out. She would be trapped walking these eternally shifting stairs alone forever. Her body ached and her eyes burned and adrenaline started to surge within her, making her stomach churn more.

'Lyssa?'

Her head snapped up, in the direction the voice had come from. 'Phyleus?'

'You're almost there,' he called back.

The relief hit her so hard she physically felt it. Renewed energy pulsed through her legs and she picked up her pace, taking two steps at a time as the section of staircase she was on swung out and joined a new, steeper part.

There he was. At the top of the steep steps Phyleus was grinning at her, and she thought his laughing brown eyes were the best things she had ever seen.

18

LYSSA

'I thought I was never going to get out,' she breathed as she reached the top step.

'We've only been in here for a minute,' he told her, pulling her towards an intricately carved arched door. The chequered floor continued to wobble beneath her.

'A minute?' she said incredulously.

'Dionysus is god of madness. There's rooms like this all over the palace and time is weird in all of them.' He gestured at the door. 'Go ahead,' he said.

She pushed open the door and was relieved to see no black and white. It was a warm room and, like the dining hall they had eaten in, it seemed to be carved from the actual tree. Fairy lights hovered everywhere, illuminating a crowd of people lining each side of the room. Four flame dishes stood in front of a throne raised on a dais. Dionysus stood up from the throne when she stepped into the room and spread his arms wide.

'Captain Lyssa!' The images flickering in the flame dishes caught her attention and she stepped towards them. Eryx and Antaeus were in the first one, huddled in the corner of a stall opposite a beautiful sleek black cat that was pacing back and forth. Hedone and Theseus were in the next one, Theseus sat on the forest floor, Hedone trying desperately to pull him to his feet. As her eyes fell on the third she recoiled, stepping backwards involuntarily. The stall was covered in blood, and the remains of a creature were scattered around the small room. Hercules was crouching in the middle of the carnage, rocking, with his hands over his face. Evadne was sat in the corner with her knees drawn up to her pale face, blood indistinguishable from the red of her dress.

Lyssa pulled her eyes away from the harrowing scene to the fourth flame dish. Her own face, covered in dirty smudges and surrounded by wild red curls, looked back at her. As she watched, a golden crown of leaves grew around her head.

'We have a victor!' roared Dionysus and the room erupted in applause.

THEY HAD WON. That was two Trials. They had won two Trials. Hope and triumph swelled in Lyssa and she stared at Phyleus.

'We won,' she said, just to hear it out loud. 'We're winning.'

'And you've won the loyalty of a chimera.' Phyleus grinned.

'About that...' Dionysus said, and the room fell quiet. 'How about I offer you a trade? Just to see what sort of hero you are.' Dionysus hopped down off the dais and stepped past the dishes towards her. She narrowed her eyes but bowed her head.

'What sort of trade?' she asked quietly.

'The madness gripping the other heroes will last some time and the memory of what they saw may haunt them for much longer. I'll end all of the madness right now and erase everyone's memory of it, including yours - in exchange for the chimera's loyalty.'

Lyssa thought of the mighty creature she'd faced in the stable, its fearsome heads and magnificent wings. Then she looked at Antaeus in the flame dish, the huge man cowering and screaming, Eryx desperate and frustrated by his side. She looked at Hedone, tears streaming down her face as she yanked at Theseus, his normally warm expression replaced by wild-eyed fear.

'I'll take your trade,' Lyssa said as she looked at the flame dish with Hercules in the centre. Her voice hardened. 'But *he* keeps the bad memories.'

'Deal,' Dionysus said. 'I'm quite happy not to do Hercules any favours. He killed my manticore, and I was quite fond of it.' The god scowled for a second then his face brightened. 'You're a smuggler - do you know where I can get a new one?'

Phyleus stepped forward.

'I'm sorry, my lord Dionysus,' he said, 'we don't trade in living beings. It's against the code.'

Lyssa looked at him, and despite herself her heart swelled with pride. Phyleus really was one of them now.

HEPHAESTUS

THE IMMORTALITY TRIALS

TRIAL SIX

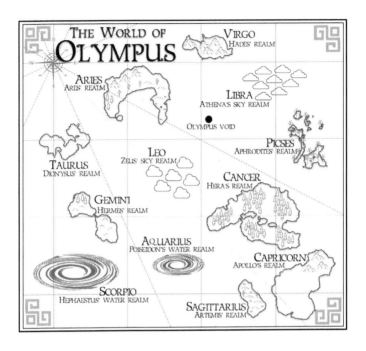

THE WORLD OF
OLYMPUS

VIRGO
HADES' REALM

ARIES
ARES' REALM

LIBRA
ATHENA'S SKY REALM

OLYMPUS VOID

PICSES
APHRODITES' REALM

TAURUS
DIONYSUS' REALM

LEO
ZEUS' SKY REALM

CANCER
HERA'S REALM

GEMINI
HERMES' REALM

AQUARIUS
POISEIDON'S WATER REALM

CAPRICORN
APOLLO'S REALM

SCORPIO
HEPHAESTUS' WATER REALM

SAGITTARIUS
ARTEMIS' REALM

1

LYSSA

'I hope you're keeping that dress on,' Phyleus said. His voice startled Lyssa as she untied the gold band from around her middle.

'Phyleus! What did I tell you about abusing talking through the ship like this?' she snapped back.

'It's important!' he protested. 'We're having a party, and that dress is perfect for a party.'

Lyssa rolled her eyes. 'Even if I wanted to keep the dress on, which I don't, it's filthy.'

There was a pause.

'You know, I could get you a new one.'

'Don't you dare. Go away.' She heard him laugh in her mind and a smile tugged at her own lips.

'You'd look great in green,' he said.

'And you'll look great hanging over the edge of the *Alastor* for dear life if you buy me a dress.'

'Captain!' Phyleus said in pretend shock. 'You wouldn't throw me overboard! Not after I just saved your life.'

'You did, you know,' she answered softly. 'Thank you.'

'You're welcome.' Lyssa could picture him shrugging.

Was he undressing in his room too? The thought made her blush. 'Oh, and in case it comes in handy, I'm immune to most madness-inducing things. Including ice-phoenix song,' he said offhandedly.

'Right. Well. That explains that.'

He said nothing, and she wiggled out of the heavy satin dress. 'What did your father make you do?' she asked him, and instantly regretted it.

There was a long pause, and she was about to apologise for prying when he said, 'He sent me to perform an ancient Taurean ritual. It's kind of a long story and... If I'm being honest, not one I'm not willing to share.'

Lyssa's face burned with embarrassment. 'I get it. Sure. I – I won't ask again,' she spluttered. Gods, how un-captain like she was being? She scrabbled for something to say that would re-assert her authority.

'Have you still got the dress on?' Phyleus said, before she could come up with anything.

'No!' she exclaimed, grateful for the change in subject.

'Oh. What have you got on?'

'None of your damn business,' she said, as a knock on her door made her swivel quickly. Was he standing outside her room? Panic filled her as she looked down at herself. She didn't have *anything* on.

'Captain?' It was Len's voice.

'Hang on,' she called out loud, with a relieved sigh. 'Len's here, so go away,' she said to Phyleus, and hurriedly pulled on trousers and a shirt from the trunk at the foot of her bed. She opened the door a fraction and looked down at the satyr.

'Len?' she said. He had a frown on his small goat face.

'Captain, you need to do something about Nestor.' Lyssa raised her eyebrows. 'She says we can't have a party.'

'Ah,' said Lyssa.

'She says it's inappropriate to celebrate.'

'She does sort of have a point,' said Lyssa. 'I mean, we're winning now, but we've still got seven more Trials to go.'

Len stamped a tiny hoof. 'All the more reason to celebrate and boost crew morale while we've got the chance!'

Lyssa sighed and looked mournfully towards her bathtub. 'Fine, I'll come and talk to her,' she said and stepped out of her room, pulling the door shut resignedly behind her.

'Nestor, I understand that it doesn't feel right to celebrate—'

'Captain, Cyllarus died and the monster who killed him is still out there,' Nestor interrupted angrily, her tail swishing hard.

'I know. And I'm sorry you've not been able to be more involved in the Trials so far. But we *are* ahead right now and that is something to celebrate.' She looked beseechingly at the centaur. 'I understand, more than anyone, that this isn't about winning. But it *is* about stopping Hercules. And we've just taken a big step towards that.' Nestor huffed. 'It's just a few drinks, maybe some music. The crew will do better in the next Trial if they get a chance to relax, I'm sure of it. We all need something to be cheerful about.'

'Fine,' said the centaur. 'But *I* shall not be celebrating until that brute is dead.' She wheeled and stamped across the planks, away from the quarterdeck. Lyssa sighed and strode to the railings. She stared out over the Palace of Elis, its deep, lush greens standing out against the soft purple sky. Should she celebrate while Hercules was still alive? The truth was, she didn't even know if they could stop him winning, let alone actually kill him. She'd been running all these years, chasing freedom in the skies, knowing deep down that she could never truly rest. Would Hercules's death change that? Or would preventing him from living forever be enough?

'So this mind-talking thing works off the ship as well?' Phyleus's voice cut through her thoughts again.

'For gods' sakes, Phyleus, stop it! Go and bother Abderos or something!'

'There's no point talking to Abderos like this, I share a room with him,' he answered.

'There's no point talking to me like this, I'm not bloody listening,' she snapped.

'Bet I could make you listen...' he said, and there was no mistaking the flirtatious tone. She gritted her teeth, the memory of his lips on hers flashing through her mind.

'The party starts soon. Until then, leave me alone,' she said.

'Got it. Don't annoy you until the party. I look forward to it.'

2

LYSSA

'Epizon?' Lyssa projected his name as a question.

'Cargo deck,' he answered immediately. She headed to the hauler, unsurprised that he was down there. He was sitting on the large wooden crate opposite Tenebrae's tank, staring at the creature thoughtfully. Tenebrae turned slowly to look at Lyssa as she pulled herself up next to Epizon.

'IT STILL WORRIES ME, you being down here alone with her,' she said.

'I don't think she's dangerous,' Epizon replied.

'Tell that to Lady Lamia,' Lyssa snorted.

'That's different. That woman was a monster.'

Lyssa thought of the decayed flesh and grimaced.

'So. Two Trials won. The *Alastor* in the lead.' She grinned at her first mate and he grinned back.

'Told you we could do it, Captain,' he said.

'Do you really think we can? We had a bit of an unexpected advantage in that last one.'

'Not just the last one. That phoenix song would have kept us both in the garden in Capricorn for the rest of time. Phyleus has turned out to be your secret weapon.' Epizon looked sideways at her as he spoke.

She shrugged. 'You were right. It was worth taking a chance on him.'

'The *Alastor* has accepted him,' Epizon said.

'So he's bothering you with mind talk too?' she asked.

'Probably not as much as you,' Epizon chuckled.

She raised her eyebrows. 'What do you mean?'

'Lyssa,' Epizon said, shifting on the crate to face her. She frowned apprehensively at his use of her name. 'It's OK if you like him. You are allowed to, you know.'

'Don't be stupid,' she said, scowling and turning back to Tenebrae. The creature's intense green eyes stared back.

'Phyleus is strong; stronger than he looks if the last few Trials are anything to go by. He's not afraid of you, and I don't believe he has any agenda.'

'You don't believe anyone has any agenda,' she shot back. 'He told me today that he has things he wants to keep secret.'

'Everybody has things they want to keep secret,' Epizon said gently. Lyssa huffed.

'Len doesn't. It would be a gift if that satyr kept more to himself,' she muttered.

Epizon laughed.

'Nestor doesn't think we should be celebrating,' Lyssa said, changing the subject.

'She's a warrior,' Epizon said, his voice full of admiration. 'They don't celebrate until the battle is won.'

'Hmm. Did you see her with those cyclopes? Gods, she can fight.'

'I know. Hopefully she can make a difference in the next

Trial.' Lyssa swung her legs against the crate. 'Where do you think the next one will be? We still have three forbidden realms to go.'

'I don't know,' Epizon shrugged. 'Hopefully it's something physical.'

Lyssa nodded. 'Hercules is good at the physical ones too,' she said quietly.

'We're better. And now we have three fighters. He's only one man.'

Lyssa looked at Epizon, drawing his words into her memory, to call on when she needed them. 'He's only one man,' she repeated.

They lapsed into silence again. Lyssa's thoughts slipped quickly back to laughing brown eyes and a warm, cheeky grin. 'Epizon,' she said.

'Mmm?'

'You said Phyleus isn't afraid of me. Does that mean other men are?'

'No. I just meant...' he paused, clearly looking for the right words. 'Most men who see your temper either want to challenge you or run away from you. I think Phyleus respects who you are.'

Lyssa pulled a face. 'He has a funny way of showing it. I can't even get him to call me captain, except sarcastically.'

Epizon turned to face her, his eyes serious. 'Lyssa, I saw the longboat sail turn black in the race on Sagittarius.' Lyssa stiffened, her stomach flipping with anxiety. She didn't want to talk about this. 'If he hadn't knocked you from the mast... Do you remember it? What the Rage felt like?'

'Not really,' she lied, chewing her lip and looking away from him.

'You *must* be careful. It's the same power that flows

through Hercules. You know better than anybody that power corrupts.'

She recalled the feeling of invincibility, the freedom, the unending surge of power, and shuddered.

'What's that got to do with Phyleus?' she asked, desperate to talk about anything but her Rage.

'Things might have ended very differently if he wasn't there.'

'You'd have done the same,' she said.

'I know, but I won't always be by your side, not like a lover would be.'

Lyssa gave a strangled cough at the word *lover* and felt her face burn. It was like talking to a family member about sex.

'I don't think Phyleus bought his way onto the *Alastor* to be my lover,' she said, refusing to look at Epizon. 'I think immortality had something to do with it.'

'Right. So that kiss was just about poisoned wine, was it?' Epizon teased.

'Why are all these damn Trials shown to everybody?' she snapped. But her stomach flipped again as she thought of those soft, full lips.

3

HEDONE

Hedone looked over her shoulder warily as she unhooked the longboat from its tether at the prow of the *Virtus*. If she was caught taking the little boat she would tell them that she was going to fly over the other kingdoms of Taurus, to see the tree-houses. It would be easier if nobody knew she'd gone anywhere, though. She willed her mind into the longboat and it floated gently away from the ship. No doubt Hercules was still moored somewhere nearby, but it might take a her a little while to find him.

The *Alastor* was a small shape in the distance, its sails gleaming against the teal-and-purple sky. It was unlikely he would be anywhere near that ship. She guided the boat in the opposite direction and picked up speed. What if he had decided to guess where the next Trial would be, instead of heeding Dionysus's instructions to stay nearby until tomorrow? Her breath caught and her heart clenched at the thought. She had to see him. Simply had to.

She zigzagged through the pastel clouds over Taurus and thought she may actually burst when she finally saw a ship with shining metal cladding hovering in the distance. She sped towards it, letting out a massive sigh of relief when she got close enough to see *Hybris* etched on the side of the Whirlwind. She was finally going to see him.

As her little boat approached the massive warship she steered around to the huge glass windows under the quarterdeck. He had told her about the full-length glass wall in his bedroom when he had visited her own quarters. A thrill ran through her when she thought about the bed Hercules slept in every night, and about sharing that bed with him. She prayed that he was in his rooms as she drew level with the beautiful windows.

She edged the boat as close to the glass as she could and peered in. The rooms were as lavish as she had thought they would be, with rich mahogany walls and red material draping and softening all the furniture, including the enormous bed. She couldn't see Hercules but there were large double doors at the back, behind the bed. Hopefully he was in one of those adjoining rooms. She knocked tentatively on the window. Nothing happened and with her heart hammering she tried again, louder.

Movement in the dark room beyond caught her eye and she held her breath. *Please, please, please be Hercules, not Evadne.* The thought of the blue-haired girl made a jealous anger prick at Hedone. She wasn't naive enough to think that Hercules wasn't sharing his bed in her absence, but she didn't want to see evidence of the fact first-hand.

The figure that filled the doorway was far too big to be Evadne, though, and desire completely overcame Hedone as Hercules stepped into the light of the windows. His eyes widened then shone as he saw her through the glass. He was at the glass in a heartbeat, pulling on a small lever, then pushing the window wide open.

'Hedone,' he breathed. 'You're here.' There was wonder in his voice and Hedone practically threw herself from the tiny longboat into his massive arms. No more words passed between them as he carried her to his bed and they sank down into the sheets together.

'So, this is Ati?' Hedone carefully stroked one hand over the cat's hairless head as she jumped up on the bed. She folded her legs underneath herself, closed her eyes slowly, then began a rumbling purr.

'She likes you.' Hercules smiled, running a lazy hand along her bare ribs.

'Hercules?' asked Hedone.

'Mmmm?' He responded, drowsily.

'I need to ask you something.' She wiggled her naked body closer against him, wanting to offset the awkwardness of the question she needed answered.

His arm tightened around her. 'Anything,' he said.

'Why did you not help Busiris escape from the cage on Capricorn?' She felt him stiffen behind her and for a moment she was terrified that she'd been too bold, but then he relaxed and took a long breath in.

'I know the gods have presented the Trials as a game,' he said quietly. 'But I must take them as seriously as life or death. We all entered this competition fully aware of the dangers. The Trials should be no less than deadly, given the prize.' He pulled gently on her shoulder, rolling her to face him. She looked into his stormy eyes, transfixed by the power burning in them. 'Immortality, Hedone. A chance to live forever.' He spoke slowly, his voice filled with determination. 'It is my duty to prove my strength to the world. They have accused me of being without mercy in the past and I see no reason not to fulfil the role Olympus has carved out for me.'

His eyes hardened and Hedone's heart went out to him. Some had called him a monster when he was on trial for what Hera had made him do. Hedone knew from her experience with her own gift that a man's mind was not his own when possessed by the will of a god. Hercules had had everything taken from him, had been the victim of a jealous goddesses' rage. She understood his bitterness. More than that, she knew she could help heal him.

'And when you are immortal, will you stay in that role?' She touched his face as she spoke, running her fingers down his short coarse beard. He looked deep into her eyes.

'When I am immortal I shall do whatever I please. And you shall be beside me.' A delicious thrill shuddered through Hedone at his words. 'We will need to plan you moving to the crew of the *Hybris* carefully, though,' he said.

Hedone frowned. 'Join the... *Hybris*?' She had been so transfixed on the short term, so determined to see Hercules and to ensure his well-being, that the practicalities of being with him after the Trials hadn't really sunk in. 'Yes, yes, I suppose I would have to leave the *Virtus*,' she said slowly.

This time Hercules frowned. 'Do you not want to?'

'I want to be wherever you are. I *will* be wherever you are.' Hercules leaned forwards and kissed her, softly at first and his gentleness took her breath away. But as she kissed him back his intensity grew, pulling his body against hers and pushing his hand into her thick dark hair. Yes. She would be wherever he was.

4

HERCULES

Soon, Hercules thought as he watched Hedone's chest move gently up and down as she slept. Soon, she would be in his bed every night. He couldn't see any other way of living. She must be beside him. But he wasn't stupid. He needed to be careful. Lyssa had won the last Trial because she had had less wine, clear and simple. Anyone with a Taurean royal on their crew would have won easily; it didn't worry him that she was winning for now. The real threat was, and always had been, Theseus. And stealing Hedone away from the *Virtus* was a sure way to attract attention and trouble that, while he could deal with it, wasn't necessary yet.

He reached out and gently touched Hedone's black hair, fanned out on the pillow. An image of red hair, red skin, red blood, flashed through his mind unbidden and he snatched his hand back. He bared his teeth and hissed as he shook his head. Damn these visions! They still plagued him even though the effects of the wine had long since worn off. The respite he had just experienced with Hedone was clearly only temporary.

He rolled silently out of the bed and padded into his living room. At the bar he poured himself a long glass of ouzo, then downed it in one gulp. It wasn't the best way to flush out the poison, but it was the most pleasurable and the most likely to help him sleep. Returning to his bedroom, he eased himself onto the mattress, not wanting to wake Hedone. She was tangled up in the silk sheets, looking breathtakingly beautiful, and he inhaled her scent and smiled as he laid his own head down on a pillow. It was time to rest.

He closed his eyes. *Red hair. Red blood.* He opened his eyes again. Hera had made him do it and Megara had got what she deserved, he told himself. Hera had made him stronger. Untouchable. He closed his eyes again. *Blood staining his hands, those hands on his face...*

It was no good. Sleep would not come. Hercules rolled over and ran his hand lightly down Hedone's arm, and she twitched and murmured as her eyes fluttered open slowly. He moved his hand to her stomach and Hedone's sleepy gaze focused on him, then she smiled, her soft lips parting. When he leaned over and kissed her, she pushed herself against his body and she filled his mind completely.

5

LYSSA

Lyssa leaned both elbows on the railings of the *Alastor*, swirling her wine around her glass as she stared out at the sky. She could still just make out the green treetops of Taurus below them, but those seemed insignificant compared to the huge rolling, swirling clouds that surrounded her ship, orange and pink. Tiny slivers of glittering dust corkscrewed among them like shooting stars.

'It is a shame that you didn't keep the dress on,' said Phyleus as he leaned against the railing beside her.

Lyssa rolled her eyes. 'Not really my style,' she said, looking sideways at him.

'Well, maybe it should be.'

'Phyleus, you're not going to turn me into a noble lady. Never going to happen.'

'You can wear a dress and still be you, you know. Your clothes don't define you.'

Lyssa heard the veiled accusation in his words. She had

judged him because he was part of a world of wealth. She wrinkled her nose.

'You weren't wearing any shoes when I met you,' she said. Phyleus laughed, loudly, and Lyssa found a smile spreading across her own face.

He stood straight and held up his glass. 'A toast? From bare feet to immortality.'

Lyssa grinned and clinked her glass against his.

'From bare feet to immortality,' she repeated and took a long drink.

'Where's Epizon?' asked Phyleus.

'Is he not up on deck?' Lyssa frowned.

Phyleus shook his head 'I haven't seen him.'

There was a jarring sound and both of them spun around, wine sloshing out of Phyleus's glass and onto the wooden planks at his feet. Lyssa groaned loudly.

'Oh gods, Len is going to play.' Phyleus raised his eyebrows in question. 'He's the only one with any skill at all on a fiddle. He says as a satyr he has a god-given ability to play but I'll let you decide if he's got that right.'

'I can play,' Phyleus said.

'Of course you can,' Lyssa drawled.

Phyleus gave her an exasperated look. 'I thought we were moving past this! We literally just had a conversation about not judging somebody by their upbringing.'

Lyssa threw both her hands in the air.

'OK, OK, I'm sorry. Please.' She gestured to where Len was sitting under the main mast next to Abderos, trying incompetently to extract a tune from the small instrument. 'Save us from this pain.'

Phyleus narrowed his eyes at her, then strode over to the satyr. Lyssa leaned back on the railings to watch. The part of her that still resented Phyleus wanted him to make a fool of himself. But a larger part of her just wanted to watch him.

'May I?' Phyleus held his hand out towards the instrument and Len looked up at him.

'Please, gods, tell me you are better than him,' said Abderos, tipping his own wine down his throat. 'We don't have enough alcohol on board to deal with him playing for long.'

Len snorted loudly, his furry face scrunching up. 'You just don't appreciate true talent when you hear it. Among my own people music like this is a gift.'

'As a fellow Taurean I can tell that satyrs would enjoy your playing. Perhaps human ears just can't hear the same things as you can,' Phyleus said diplomatically. Lyssa smiled as Len straightened slightly and passed the instrument to Phyleus, nodding.

'Yes. I'm sure that's what it is...' Abderos started to speak but Phyleus's drew the bow across the instrument's strings and his words faded.

Phyleus had been right. He could play. The tune wasn't exactly melancholy but neither was it uplifting. Grief and love swelled within Lyssa as the chords flowed and she watched Phyleus sway as he played. The delicate start of the piece had been misleading, and the longer he played the more the tune built. Power seem to flow through the notes and they pulled at something deep inside her.

It wasn't sadness she was feeling, but resolution. A determination to make amends for all the wrong that she and her crew had been dealt. As the tune reached a crescendo Lyssa realised she was holding her breath. Phyleus was moving around the deck now, his steps in time with the powerful music, his eyes closed. He was beautiful. The curves of his arms as he drew the bow backwards and forwards, his lithe frame moving in time to the music. She wanted him. The notes built and built and as they did, so did her desire.

Phyleus opened his eyes as he played the final climactic note. There was a moment's silence, then everyone on the deck erupted into applause. Even Nestor, who had been standing solemnly apart from the group, moved forwards, her hands clapping and face soft. Lyssa stepped away from the railing towards Phyleus.

'That was...' she started. His eyes were shining, his lips parted, his chest heaving. She could see the thrill he'd got from playing. He looked so alive. Heat burned inside her and her skin prickled. 'That was... really good,' she finished carefully. He smiled.

'How about something more appropriate for a party?' he said, and began to play again, this time an upbeat melody that made Lyssa want to tap her feet. Len made a small noise of delight, leaped off his box and grabbed Lyssa's hand. She laughed as he twirled under her arm, an easy thing to do given that he only reached her hip. She caught Phyleus's eyes and his voice sounded in her head.

'Dance, Captain Lyssa. Dance like there's no tomorrow.'

And she did.

6

EVADNE

E vadne had needed to do little to avoid her captain since they'd been back on board the *Hybris,* but she'd barely left her room all the same. She paced back and forth, unable to read or sleep. Every time she pictured his face she saw that maniacal look in his eyes, felt the hot blood of the manticore splatter across her face. She felt trapped, her ambition and need to win warring with her instinctual sense of self-preservation. Hercules was dangerous, of that there was no doubt.

The walls of her small chambers seemed to close in around her, her options limited and her mind unable to settle. Suddenly feeling like she couldn't breathe, she kicked open the door and half-ran to the hauler. She needed air.

As soon as she got to the top deck she headed for the railings, taking a long breath and trying to calm her skittering stomach. How long would it take for Hercules to go too far with her punishments? Where would she go if she had to escape? Would he follow her if she ran? Could she really flee and give up the chance to win immortality? The endless questions whirled through her brain.

She gripped the rail and closed her eyes. There was always another way. There was always another option. She just needed to find it. Her eyes fluttered open as a thought struck her.

IT WAS A RISK, taking the longboat, but she was sure she could come up with some sight-seeing explanation if she was caught.

It took her no time at all to find the massive Zephyr floating almost directly above the Palace of Elis. Knowing now where Eryx's chambers were, it was easy to draw her longboat alongside his rooms. There he was, shirtless and scrubbing at his face with a flannel over a small bowl in the corner of the room. His dark hair was out of its knot and hung to his broad shoulders. She watched him a moment then rapped on the glass, his jump of surprise making her smile. He hurried over to the window, which was a porthole bigger than she was, but she supposed small for a giant, and swung it open.

'What are you doing here?' he hissed.

'What kind of greeting is that? Aren't you going to invite me in?' Evadne cooed. She cocked her head at him and folded her arms under her chest, knowing what it did to her breasts. His eyes flicked down, his cheeks reddened and he stepped back.

'Please don't make me regret this,' he said as she stood up in the boat, put both hands on the porthole rim and pulled herself through the hole. She landed relatively gracefully, then straightened, brushing herself off needlessly. 'Why are you here?' Eryx demanded, gathering his hair back up and tying a band around it quickly.

'I just... I just needed to get off the *Hybris* for a while. I didn't know where else to go,' Evadne said quietly. It was the truth, she realised as she spoke it. Whether or not she would find a shot at immortality on this ship instead of Hercules's, she really didn't have anywhere else to go.

Eryx's scarred face softened. For a moment he looked like he would step towards her but then he seemed to change his mind, his foot lifting and falling back into place. She saw the long pink scar on his chest and reached her own hand out towards it.

'This is healing well,' she said. He grunted, eyeing her hand warily.

'Your crew were the only ones who were going to leave Busiris to die,' he said abruptly.

Evadne let loose a long breath and sat down heavily on the end of Eryx's bed. 'I know. I... I misjudged my captain,' she said and put her head in her hands.

Eryx stepped towards her. 'So you would *not* have left him to die?'

She looked up at him. 'I asked Hercules to go back. I asked him to help. He punished me.' Anger flashed across the half-giant's face and something sparked inside Evadne. It had been a long time since anyone had felt indignation or anger on her behalf.

'He punished you?'

'Yes. He made me scrub the decks.'

Eryx barked out a laugh.

'We have to scrub the deck on the *Orion* as a daily chore, not a punishment.'

Evadne shrugged. 'What can I say? I was brought up a princess.' She gave him a sarcastic smile as he gaped.

'A princess?'

This time Evadne laughed and stood up, shaking her head. 'Not a real one, you idiot. I just meant I was spoiled as a child. I didn't do much scrubbing.'

'Don't call me an idiot,' growled Eryx.

Evadne was about to tease him more but the look on his face stopped her.

'You're not an idiot, Eryx. It's just the way I speak. I'm the idiot,' she said softly. 'You can read all the books in the world, learn everything there is to know about Olympus, chase fame and fortune your whole life, but you can't control the people around you.'

Eryx stared at her. 'Why are you here?' he asked her quietly.

'I told you, I just needed to get off the *Hybris*. Talk to somebody.'

Eryx pushed his hand through his dark hair, loosening the knot he had just tied. His honest open face was so starkly different to her captain's that for a moment Evadne questioned her resolve. Should she use this man? She had to.

And she needed to play her move carefully. Swiping her hair casually back behind her ears, she turned her head under the pretence of looking around the room, knowing it would expose the bruises still on her neck.

'He hurts you, doesn't he.' It wasn't a question. Eryx's face darkened and his fists clenched at his sides and she found herself distracted by the muscles rippling across his chest as he tensed.

'It's nothing I can't handle. The *Hybris* is just not a nice place to be at the moment. Lyssa winning is not good for him.'

Eryx said nothing, just flexed his balled fists.

. . .

SHE STARED AT HIM, thinking. She had done what she needed to do. Should she ever need refuge from Hercules, Eryx would be prepared to help her, she was sure of it.

Then why didn't she want to leave?

'Do you have any dice?' she asked him.

His eyebrows shot up. 'Dice? You want to... play dice?'

'Sure.' She shrugged and sat back down on his bed. 'You got anything better to do?'

A small smile crossed his face.

'I have dice. But I don't know how to play much.'

'I'll teach you,' she said.

THEY PLAYED for the best part of two hours, before Evadne began to worry that she would be missed. The flash of disappointment on Eryx's broad face when she announced that she was leaving caused that spark within her to fire again. He wanted her company. The feeling was nice.

'You should have left ages ago,' Eryx said, the words conflicting with his expression. She walked to the window, which at head height for him was high for her. He crouched beside her, creating a cradle with his hands, and she put one boot into it, resting both her other hands on his shoulder. His head was now level with her abdomen and she felt him stiffen before he lifted her easily up to the porthole.

'Thank you, Eryx,' she said as she pulled herself through the window and landed lightly in the longboat. She leaned back through and touched a hand to his cheek, surprised by the real emotion she saw and felt when she did so. She wouldn't hurt this man, she decided. If he could help her, she would use him, but she wouldn't hurt him. She pulled her arm back and willed her boat forwards, not turning back to look at him.

As she rounded the hull of the boat, though, she saw Busiris standing by the railings. His glittering black eyes were fixed on her as she sailed past.

7

ERYX

When Eryx awoke, Evadne's face filled his mind. He had dreamed of her.

He groaned and buried his face in his pillow. This would get him nowhere; he had to stop thinking about her. Why would a tiny, young thing like her be interested in a big old brute like him? Eryx knew there were a lot of folk out there who were smarter than he was, but he wasn't stupid enough to believe that she didn't have ulterior motives. But that touch... The look in her eyes. It felt so real.

'Eryx, the announcement's in less than half an hour. You should be up on the quarterdeck.' Antaeus's voice thundered through his thoughts and he swung his legs out of bed quickly, grateful for the distraction.

'Who do you think it's going to be?' Eryx asked the group in general. They were once again huddled around the flame dish, waiting to find out what they would be facing next. Nobody answered him. 'Well, it can't be as bad as the last one,' he said. Antaeus grunted. After two particularly bad Trials they were due a break, Eryx thought.

The flames suddenly leaped, flashing white, and everyone breathed in and leaned forwards.

'Good morning, Olympus!' The irritating blond announcer beamed. 'So, we have a crew out in front! Captain Lyssa and the *Alastor* have now won two Trials. All the other crews have one, and there's still plenty of time to catch up.' Eryx frowned at the small man. 'So let's give you that chance with no further delay! Here's your next host...' He faded away, then the image refocused on a hulking, stooped, oily figure with dark hair and a creased face. Hephaestus.

A thrill ran through Eryx. Although they were all sons of Poseidon, giants were one of the few races allowed in Hephaestus's forbidden realm, Scorpio. It was known as a haven for giants, cyclopes and other brutish species that could work in his forges. Eryx had never had trouble finding work fighting as a boxer but the knowledge of that potential haven had carried him, and many like him, through doubtful times.

'Heroes,' Hephaestus grunted, his bushy beard lopsided on his ugly face. 'I have designed and built a new monster for you to tackle in Scorpio. It is called a stymphalian bird. If you can disable three of these birds you will win. If you can reach the birds' nest and take one of their eggs you may keep it.

'As you are aware, my realm is under water, so you will be given the ability to breathe water for the duration of the Trial. I will only grant this to two people on your crew, however. When all ships have reached Scorpio you will be transported to the starting point.' The image shimmered and Hephaestus disappeared.

'More water,' said Antaeus, quietly.

'It won't be cold this time,' said Busiris. 'I have visited Hephaestus's forges before and the ocean surrounding them is temperate.'

Antaeus looked at the gold-skinned giant. 'Do you want to partake in this Trial?' he asked him.

Busiris stared back a moment, then shook his head. 'No, Captain. I do not believe I am best placed for this. There is little water in the desert and my swimming will not be the strongest on this crew.'

Antaeus sighed. 'Eryx?'

Eryx's heart started to pound and he raised his eyebrows hopefully as his captain looked at him. 'You swim both well and fast. Are you up for another Trial?'

Eryx nodded enthusiastically.

'Of course, Captain.'

SCORPIO WAS ONLY HALF a day due south of Taurus, and Eryx spent the time exercising. He moved and twisted, rolled and jumped on the huge Zephyr deck, taking great care not to let any discomfort from his chest wound show when any of his crew-mates were about. Neither Albion or Bergion liked being in the water so there was no resentment over Antaeus's choice of partner. Rather, they both clapped him on the back and wished him luck.

IT WAS easy to spot Scorpio in the vast ocean, due to the huge spiralling pillars of steam erupting from the water's surface. Unsurprisingly, the Zephyr was the last ship there. The *Hybris*, *Virtus* and *Alastor* were already hovering ten feet above the glittering ocean.

'Are you ready?' said Antaeus as the boat came to a halt with the others.

Eryx nodded. There was a flash of light and they were no longer on the *Orion*.

ERYX'S MOUTH fell open as he took an involuntary step backwards and gaped around him.

They were inside a volcano. A towering structure made up of spires, bridges and rocky platforms, all carved from a dark rough stone, lined the inside of the hollow mountain. Fiercely bright, deep orange liquid poured in rivulets down channels in the rock, pooling in huge vats or running all the way to the bottom, where they were standing on the banks of a pool of the molten lava. Eryx looked up, and though he could just see the top of the volcano, billowing white steam made it impossible to see the ocean beyond. Sweat trickled down into his eyes as he peered up. The hot air was filled with metallic clanging and hammering, then Hephaestus's voice boomed and echoed through the volcano.

'Find your way out of the forge. There are many exits in the sides of the volcano. Kill the birds.'

With wise Athena Hephaestus taught many creatures amazing crafts, creatures who before lived in caves on mountains like wild beasts. Since learning skills from Hephaestus the metalworker though, they have a peaceful life and somewhere to live for good.

EXCERPT FROM

HOMERIC HYMN 20 TO HEPHAESTUS

Written 7–4 BC

Paraphrased by Eliza Raine

8

LYSSA

L yssa grabbed Epizon's elbow, pulling him back as the others raced towards the rock steps behind them.

Epizon raised his eyebrows at her. 'What's wrong, Captain?'

'There's a smaller set of steps over there,' Lyssa said, pointing to their right, where a huge arching bridge jutted out over the pool of lava, far above them. Concealed in the shadow of the tall foot of the bridge it was just possible to make out a small staircase.

They jogged towards it, Lyssa wishing dearly that she'd worn a sleeveless shirt. It was almost unbearably hot in the forge. Sweat was pooling in the small of her back already.

They reached the stairs and found that the steps were carved into the bridge itself. As they began to make their way up, Lyssa realised that it wasn't rock that they were walking on, but hardened lava, the surface glittering in the flickering orange light. By the time they reached the barrier-less bridge sweat was dripping down Lyssa's face and neck.

A thundering clank made her jump as she paused for

breath, and she turned in the direction of the noise. Flush with the wall of the volcano was one of the massive vats collecting the liquid fire that ran down the walls. Out of the vat jutted a series of flat, dull anvils and at each of them worked a telkhine. She had seen the creatures before, in books and also at the feast, but the sight of them here in the forge made her stare.

Although they were mostly reminiscent of human-sized dogs, they had weirdly webbed hands that seemed like they would be clumsy. Yet telkhines were famously Olympus's most magnificent smiths. Instead of back legs and a tail like a dog's, they had something more like a fish tail, short and squat. The four telkhines Lyssa could see now were propped up on the base of their tails, their webbed hands either heaving massive hammers or manipulating lumps of metal, still glowing from heat.

Was Tenebrae related to the telkhines? Lyssa cocked her head, wondering. Tenebrae's tail looked nothing like theirs, though, and her head was more humanoid than their canine ones.

A pair of glowing white eyes locked on hers, and the telkhine's fast fingers paused. Lyssa looked away and began to hurry across the bridge.

'Aren't they amazing?' breathed Epizon.

'They're ugly as sin,' answered Lyssa.

'But, Captain, the things they can create—'

'Concentrate, Epizon. We need a way out of this volcano,' Lyssa cut him off. If they could win one more Trial, they would be comfortably in the lead.

'Yes, Captain.'

She tried not to look down as they raced along the bridge. Rising above them on either side were curved spires of lava rock, orange light glowing through holes dotting

their surface. Were these the homes of the creatures that
lived in the forge?

They reached the other side of the volcano and Lyssa's
heart sank as she saw another vat of lava surrounded by
working creatures, this time three cyclopes.

'What did Hephaestus mean, there are plenty of ways
out of the sides?' she snapped, slowing down.

'Check the walls,' said Epizon, his head moving from
side to side as he scanned the rock.

'The only holes I can see from here are the ones the
lava's flowing from.'

Epizon looked slowly at her. She shook her head. 'No
way.'

Epizon shrugged. 'Maybe. It wouldn't be the worst thing
we've experienced on a Trial so far.'

She stared at him. 'How is climbing through a hole filled
with running lava not the worst thing we've experienced so
far?'

'OK, it is pretty bad,' her first mate conceded.

Lyssa huffed angrily. 'Right. I guess we'd better go and
look at one of these holes, then,' she hissed, and jogged
towards the next set of stairs embedded in the rock wall.

THEY HAD ONLY GOT up to the next platform when they
saw Hercules, running with Evadne towards them. They
all slowed, crackling tension cutting through the
humid air.

'Captain,' Epizon mumbled a warning behind her. 'Concentrate, remember,' he said. But Lyssa didn't hear him.
Hercules's cold grey eyes had locked on hers and anger was
already bubbling through her.

'Daughter,' he said as they reached each other.

'I told you not to call me that,' she spat, her fists clenching and her skin stinging.

Hercules tilted his head at her.

'But you are my daughter, it's obvious now. It is clearly my blood in your veins, and you have an extraordinary amount of luck, or you would already be dead,' he said icily, stepping closer to her.

'Keep telling yourself that, and I'll keep winning.' Blood was pounding in her ears and fear was hammering at the anger, threatening to make her step back, away from him. She forced her legs to stay still, forced her heaving stomach to settle. She didn't need to be afraid of him any more.

His lips curled up in a sick smile and her composure faltered as memories flashed in front of her, unbidden. She took a ragged breath and he laughed softly, close enough now that she could feel his hot breath on her face.

'I'm not only going to beat you, daughter, I am going to win. I will be immortal, and you will die.' His voice was like a million knives ripping through her. He would kill her. He had been ready to four years ago. He had already killed her family... Fear froze her muscles, the Rage pounding against a wall of terror inside her.

He laughed again and stepped back. 'Poor little Lyssa,' he said, and strode past her.

Hot tears pricked her eyes as she stood stock still, not daring to move yet.

'Has he gone?' she whispered.

'Yes, Captain,' Epizon said and laid a hand on her shoulder. She flinched and he tightened his grip. 'He's gone.'

She turned to him, frustration and anger overwhelming her.

'How can I beat him like this? How? I'm still so bloody scared of him!' The admission burst from her mouth and she immediately hated herself for saying it out loud. She fixed her stare on the rock at her feet, willing the angry tears not to spill from her eyes.

'He's one man, Lyssa, and you're already beating him.' She looked at Epizon. 'Athena thinks you can win and you're already proving her right. Hercules just practically admitted that you're a threat to him. He should be scared of you.' Epizon smiled at her and she gave him a small one back. 'Come on. We need to get out of this volcano.' He gave her shoulder a squeeze, then walked slowly past her, continuing towards the lava fall. Lyssa took a long breath, her fists still clenched so hard that her nails were biting into the skin of her palms.

She was no longer the girl who ran. And she hadn't run, even though she'd wanted to. She had stood her ground. Athena thought she could beat Hercules. She *had* to beat him.

EPIZON HAD BEEN RIGHT about the lava holes. And it wasn't as bad as she had thought it would be. The holes were massive, easily big enough for a giant to fit through. The rock was rough enough that it was not difficult to climb above the slow-moving flow of fiery liquid, where they found a long ledge running along the shaft.

The lava flowed down from a vertical tunnel about twenty feet into the tube, and when they reached it she pressed herself flat to the wall, carefully inching her way past the waterfall of lava. The heat was fierce, forcing her to squeeze her eyes shut until she was past. When she opened them again, she gasped. There was a wall of water at the end of the tunnel. She held her hand out in amazement as she reached it, touching the ebbing, rippling surface.

'What do you think it's going to be like, being able to breathe under water?' she whispered.

'Slightly alarming at first, I imagine,' answered Epizon.

'Huh.'

'Let's find out, Captain,' he said.

Lyssa nodded and took a long step off the ledge and through the wall of water.

The Arabian desert is home to Stymphalian birds which are as dangerous to men as lions or leopards. They fly at those who hunt them and wound them with their powerful straight beaks and are the size of a crane.

EXCERPT FROM

DESCRIPTION OF GREECE BY PAUSANIAS

Written 2 AD

Paraphrased by Eliza Raine

9

HEDONE

Hedone held her breath as she stepped through the wall of water, into the ocean beyond. She couldn't help it, it was instinctual.

Delicious coolness washed over her hot skin as her eyes widened. The floor of the ocean was not far beneath them and it was carpeted in vivid life. Rocky outcrops covered in bright plants and tiny colourful fish dotted a blanket of dark green moss. Her lungs started to burn and as she realised she needed air a flash of panic gripped her.

It's OK, she told herself. *Hephaestus said we would be able to breathe, we'll be able to breathe. Take a breath*, she commanded herself. But her body refused to obey.

She looked around wildly for Theseus and caught sight of his dark skin in her peripheral vision. She spun in the water, focusing on her captain's bare chest as he hovered in place before her. He waved calmly at her and took a very long, obvious breath. He was doing it! He was breathing under water. Chest aching, Hedone closed her eyes and breathed in.

The water did not even enter her mouth. She felt clear

cool air filling her lungs and laughed aloud in relief, her eyebrows rising in surprise when she realised that she couldn't hear her own voice. Theseus drew his hand across his neck repeatedly, the meaning clear. They would not be able to speak.

SUDDENLY SOMETHING SILVER shot down between them, the water moving so hard it rocked both of them backwards. She followed the projectile's motion until it thudded into the gargantuan volcano they had just emerged from, and gasped. It was a metal spike, shaped like a blade, the size of her forearm.

She craned her neck in the opposite direction, trying to see where it had come from, and her face contorted. The water was crystal clear and between the brightly lit surface, where she could see the shadows of the four ships above, was a huge flock of metal birds. A few of them were darting out of the group towards them and she could see them clearly as they fired metal feathers at her and Theseus from their angular wings.

Except for their silver wing feathers they were a gleaming brass colour and almost as large as she was. They had tiny black eyes set in bulbous heads and short sharp beaks that quickly snapped open and closed as their wings propelled them through the water.

Theseus grabbed her arm and pulled her downwards, breaking her mesmerised stare. She swam fast with him, towards the busy ocean floor. How were they going to kill three of these beasts? How would they even get close to them? Hedone had volunteered to come not for her fighting skill but for her ability to swim. She had hoped she would be able to get to the nest while the birds were distracted by

Theseus and the other heroes. But she didn't have any idea where the nest even was, let alone if she had the courage to try to get past these vile things.

Theseus dragged them down behind a large lump of rock teeming with sea life and frowned at her. She shrugged back at him, then started as she saw movement behind him. This wasn't another silver-sharpened feather, though. It was a telkhine, she realised in surprise.

The creature hadn't seen her, and he was swimming fast along the ocean floor, darting between the outcrops. Unlike the ones in the forge, who had been wearing bronze armour and leather face gear, this telkhine was shirtless, his short dark fur plastered to his chest, and a longer mane running down the back of his neck and spine. He carried a small trident with glowing amber stone in the centre.

Hedone pointed frantically, but by the time Theseus had turned around the telkhine was gone from view.

10

ERYX

Eryx ducked once again behind a big leafy plant that rippled in the water as a metal feather sailed past. If the birds' aim had been any better the plant would have provided him with little protection.

He kicked, looking around the ocean floor for something sturdier to hide behind. Antaeus pulled at his arm and he turned. His captain pointed at the volcano and Eryx frowned. What was over there? Antaeus gave a shout that Eryx could not hear but was plain to see, then kicked away from him, towards the volcano.

Eryx swam after him, wondering what they were doing. They stuck close to the rocks as they swam, the birds' missiles mostly losing momentum by the time they reached the sea bottom. Hercules was drawing a large proportion of the fire by swimming up out of the cover of the plants on the ground, his lion-skin cloak wrapped around him.

Antaeus ignored the others, though, only stopping when he reached a tube in the side of the volcano that led back into the forge. He gripped the side and dragged himself through. Eryx followed.

. . .

THE HEAT HIT him again the moment he cleared the water, wobbling on the ledge for a second, until Antaeus gripped his shoulder and steadied him.

'What—'

'We're giants,' Antaeus growled. Eryx blinked at him. 'There's nothing that can defeat those birds, other than Hephaestus's own metal.' Eryx continued to stare at him and Antaeus closed his eyes and clenched his jaw. 'We need to find something forged in here that can kill them,' he said slowly. 'And if we can't find something, then we'll make something.'

It was genius, thought Eryx, his mouth hanging open slightly.

'Excellent idea, Captain.' He nodded and Antaeus grunted, turning to make his way back along the ledge and past the molten flow of lava.

'AREN'T YOU HOT?' asked Eryx as they ran along one of the platforms, looking for a vat tended by fellow giants. So far they had only seen telkhines and cyclopes, neither of which Antaeus thought would be as inclined to help them.

'That's the human part of you,' muttered his captain. 'Giants don't feel heat. Here!' Antaeus slowed as they approached a massive vat, with just three huge anvils attached. A giant five feet taller than Antaeus was dipping the largest hammer Eryx had ever seen into the burning lava.

'GREETINGS,' Antaeus called.

The giant was more scarred than anyone on board the *Orion*. He turned slowly towards them and scowled.

'We are looking for something that could kill a stymphalian bird,' Antaeus continued. 'Do you know of anything?'

'Nothing can kill a stymphalian bird. They are not alive.' The giant grunted and turned back to his hammer.

'Disable one, then?' Antaeus tried.

The giant paused, then turned back to them.

'You are the giant crew? The sons of Poseidon?' he asked slowly. Antaeus nodded up at him.

'We are. You have heard of us?'

The giant nodded.

'We have flame dishes here.' He stared at Antaeus for a few moments. 'I can help you make a net from the same metal they are forged from. It will work,' he said eventually.

Antaeus put his hands together and dipped his head in thanks.

'We will be indebted to you. What is your name?'

'Hyperion,' the massive man answered, dropping his glowing hammer on the ground beside him.

'I am Antaeus, and this is—'

The giant cut him off before he could introduce Eryx.

'I do not care to know the halfling's name. Come,' Hyperion said, and the platform thudded with each step he took towards a pile of metal sheets.

Eryx's face burned, but he said nothing as Antaeus looked at him, mildly apologetic.

'It is the old way, Brother,' his captain muttered quietly. 'Do not let it bother you.' He clapped him on the shoulder and trotted after Hyperion.

Eryx scowled. He would prove that a halfling was worth a name, he decided, and followed Antaeus.

11

HERCULES

A feather blade hit Hercules hard in the shoulder and he spun through the water until the light coming from the surface helped him right himself. If it weren't for the lion skin he wouldn't have survived any of the blows he had received. Every time he got past a few missiles, more would come and he was forced to back off again.

He bared his teeth, frustration and anger building in him, and swam back down to where Evadne was crouched behind a large rock, swiping at the bright fish that swarmed around it, her blue hair in a tail that floated around her head. When he glared at her she shrugged, and he lashed out at the rock.

Hundreds of fish burst from it and Evadne jumped, moving away quickly. He gestured away from the rock, trying to get her to realise she should be looking for the nest. That was the only reason she was there, the only way she could be helpful.

She followed his pointing finger and glanced nervously up at the flock of birds. With clear trepidation, she swam out from behind the rock, sticking closely to the mossy floor, and began pulling at plants and peering into holes in the rocks. It was a good job he wasn't so damn cowardly, he thought as he swam back up towards the stymphalian birds, his lion skin pulled high over his head. How would he kill them? Pulling heads off worked with most creatures, he reasoned, and the Hydra had been a metal automaton too. That monster had died.

A FLASH of red caught his eye and he turned in the water. Lyssa was kicking up, moving behind a bird that was swimming much lower than the rest of the flock. So far it hadn't noticed her, instead firing its missiles at her hulking first mate, who was darting about below them, avoiding the feathers relatively easily.

Anger swept over Hercules as he saw her reach the bird, draw back her fist and power it into the creature's shining brass head. It froze for a moment, clearly stunned, and she wrapped her arm around its neck, using her legs to pin its lethal wings to its sides. She twisted, her red hair fanning out around her at the sudden movement, and the bird went limp in her grasp. She let go of it and swam back towards the black man, pumping her fist in triumph.

Hercules's anger turned to fury. How had she, that pathetic, insignificant child, killed one of these things before he had? His muscles clenched and his fists balled as his incredulity grew. Then, suddenly, pain lanced through his calf as a feather caught his exposed leg. The memory of Lyssa shooting him in the same leg after he killed the lion, bringing him to one knee in front of the world, flashed in front of him, and Hercules roared as his vision clouded and he shot towards Lyssa.

12

EVADNE

E vadne didn't want to be roaming the ocean floor, a potential target for those lethal feathers. Her initial awe at the beauty of the underwater volcano and the vivid ocean floor had quickly been replaced by fear when she'd seen the bronze birds.

She took a shallow breath as she pulled aside the large flat leaves of yet another plant, looking for anything that resembled a nest. The salt water made her buoyant and it took little energy to hover in place. Although she'd read the water was warm in Scorpio, it still felt strange.

But she hadn't thought she would be so uncomfortable breathing under water. Try as she might, she just couldn't bring herself to take deep breaths in, it was just so unnatural.

Movement caught her eye and her attention snapped from the black-and-white striped fish in front of her, and over to her left. She saw a large dark tail as it flicked and vanished around a large rock covered in pastel-coloured growths.

Evadne frowned. Was that a fish? She kicked tentatively towards it, casting regular glances above her to ensure she did not have the attention of any of the stymphalian birds. She reached the rock, and tiny fish pulsed out from it in alarm before returning to whatever it was they had been doing before she had disturbed them. *So much for a stealthy approach*, she thought.

She swam cautiously to where she'd seen the tail disappear, but when she peered around there was nothing there. She sighed, slightly disappointed, then noticed more movement in her peripheral vision. She spun around quickly, the water pulling at her clothes, and this time she saw more than a tail. It wasn't a fish. It was a telkhine, bare-chested and fierce-looking, with a long mane that rippled as he swam between plants and rocks. Evadne moved quickly, following the creature.

HE SEEMED to be heading back towards the volcano, which unfortunately for Evadne, was also where most of the birds were. But if anybody knew where the nest was, surely it would be the natives? She didn't know if the telkhine would or could speak to her, but it seemed like a better idea than just looking behind every plant on the ocean floor.

His squat tail flicked as he swam thirty feet in front of her, swerving and weaving easily through obstacles. Her progress was much slower, not helped by constantly needing to check for sharpened feathers flying her way. She was becoming tired trying to keep up with him and her shallow breathing was making her feel worse.

When the telkhine reached the foot of the volcano he

didn't start moving up as she expected him to, but instead carried on around the base of the huge rock edifice. She would be completely out of sight of Hercules and the other heroes if she followed him, she realised.

She looked up, trying to locate the others. She could see Lyssa's red hair clearly, and it looked like she was engaged with one of the metal creatures. If she beat it and went on to win, life on the *Hybris* would be unbearable.

Evadne closed her eyes, forced herself to take a deep breath of cool dry air, and kicked her way around the mountain.

13

HEDONE

Theseus beckoned to Hedone and she moved cautiously, unwilling to venture too far from the cover of the rocky floor. Where did he want to go now?

With little other option, Hedone followed her captain as he swam, sticking low to the mossy ground, keeping her back towards the volcano. When they reached the giant rock he headed straight up, still staying close to the surface, avoiding the attention of the birds. Soon they reached one of the tubes that led back into the forge and she watched, confused but slightly relieved, as Theseus pulled himself through the hole. She quickly followed him, dropping into a crouch on the narrow ledge and breathing in the hot air heavily. Theseus leaned against the rock wall and pushed his wet hair out of his face.

'We need a new plan,' he said.

'You've got one?' She looked up at him, wringing out her own dark hair, the water cool as it dripped down her back in the stifling heat.

'These birds were made by Hephaestus, and so are most

weapons in this forge. There must be something in here we can use,' he said.

'We?' Hedone looked at him doubtfully. Almost every creature that worked in this forge was three times her size and weight. It was unlikely she would be able to wield any weapon they found in the volcano.

'Come on,' Theseus said, and held his hand out to pull her back to her feet. They edged past the waterfall of lava, the heat drying their clothes almost immediately, and emerged onto a platform next to a vat tended by four cyclopes. The creatures cast uninterested glances at them and continued hammering at enormous lumps of glowing metal.

Theseus started looking around, before jogging towards a pile of metal sheets stacked against the shadowy wall.

'What are you looking for?' Hedone asked.

'I don't know,' Theseus muttered. 'Anything that might help.'

Hedone scowled. While it was a relief to be out of the water and away from the birds, she couldn't see Hercules from inside the mountain, and didn't know if he was OK. She didn't want to be in here long.

Theseus heaved the stack of metal sheets aside, the muscles in his shoulders rippling. Hedone cocked her head. How had she ever thought him more beautiful than Hercules? He was practically puny in comparison.

There was nothing behind the sheets, and Theseus cursed quietly.

They jogged on to the next vat and pile of metal. Theseus shifted and dug through discarded lumps of misshapen steel and iron, Hedone becoming increasingly anxious to get back out into the water, until he finally exclaimed in triumph.

'Aha!' He dragged a dull iron spear upright next to him. It was at least ten feet tall and Hedone blinked up at its end, where there were three sharp prongs. It wasn't a spear, but a trident. 'This might work,' Theseus said. He hefted it onto his shoulder awkwardly, then ran for the nearest lava tube.

14

ERYX

Sweat flowed freely down Eryx's brow as he brought the hammer down on the anvil again and again. His shoulders burned from the weight of the tool, but there was no way he was going to stop. Not when Hyperion was watching him so closely.

He cast a sideways glance at Antaeus at the next anvil, the tattooed serpents on his back writhing as his muscles strained. Surely the square of metal in front of him had to be flat enough by now? He picked up it up and peered at it closely, then turned and handed it to Hyperion. The giant took it and examined every bit of the surface, then gave a tiny nod. He laid it down next to eight others, forming a larger square over a pattern moulded into the rock of the platform.

'That should be enough,' he said, and Antaeus dropped his hammer with a clang.

'Now what?' asked Eryx, trying not to pant.

Hyperion ambled to the vat and picked up what looked like a massive spoon with a long handle. He dipped it in the molten lava and carried it carefully over to the squares of metal, then began to pour. The metal hissed and glowed and melted into the carved shape below. Hyperion went to get another ladleful, three times, eventually completely covering the mould. Then he crouched down beside one corner and dipped his hands into the glowing liquid metal.

Eryx cried out and stepped forwards but Antaeus put his arm in front of him and glared. Eryx dropped his hands to his side and watched in amazement as Hyperion moved quickly, manipulating a section of the cooling metal, then moving on. In just a few minutes he had covered the whole area.

He stood up and gestured for them to approach.

It was a net. As promised. Eryx stared at the tiny links of metal, hundreds of them, all chained together into a tight, almost beautiful web.

'How...?'

'You learn much in the forges,' Hyperion said simply. 'Take it and go with luck.' He turned away without a smile and lumbered towards the stairs to a nearby bridge.

THE NET WAS SO heavy that Eryx and Antaeus could only just carry it between them. Eryx was sure that there was no part of his body not sweating when they finally set it down in front of a lava tube.

'We're going to have to roll it to get past the lava fall,' said Antaeus. Eryx grunted and they laid the net out flat on the platform, then began to roll, the small interlocking links clinking as they went.

'You really think this will work, Captain?' asked Eryx.

'I trust Hyperion,' answered Antaeus. When the net was rolled into a long flexible tube they each heaved an end over one shoulder and climbed carefully onto the ledge. They made slow progress, Eryx desperate to get back to the cooler water and longing for that surreal sensation of being to breathe clear, cool air. It was stifling in the forge. Perhaps he would have to re-evaluate his notion of Scorpio as a haven. Hyperion may have been right. His human traits did make him different.

'See you on the other side,' called Antaeus, and Eryx snapped out of his thoughts as his captain disappeared through the rippling wall of water at the end of the tube. He hurried after him, the net becoming lighter in his hands as the water took more of its weight.

THEY EMERGED high on the volcano, above a smaller group of the birds. *Perfect*, he thought, relishing the sudden lack of heat. Antaeus had hold of the edge of the net and between them they slowly unrolled it. Holding a corner each, they swam towards the metal birds, Eryx brimming with confidence.

15

LYSSA

something hard hit Lyssa out of nowhere and her cry of surprise and pain was lost as she went tumbling through the water. She kicked wildly, trying to right herself. A metal feather swished past her and she whirled around in confusion. Then Hercules was in front of her, a deadly calm on his face.

It was as though time slowed to a stop. Her body reacted, her power building inside her, and she waited for the paralysing fear to clamp around her. But it didn't come. *I am no longer the girl who ran.* The words rang loud and clear through her mind as she stared into those familiar grey eyes. It was true. She wanted to bellow the mantra in his face, scream at him that this time she would make him want to run and hide, that it was her turn to cause him pain. Red seeped into her vision and her skin throbbed with Rage as his mouth turned up in a cold smile.

LYSSA AND HERCULES launched themselves at each other

simultaneously. Gods, he was strong. Stronger than her, she realised as his shoulder caught her square in the chest. She gasped for breath as she rolled backwards, barely ducking out of his way in time as he turned and charged again.

She kicked hard through the water to get above him and threw her hands out at his neck. Her right hand made contact and she dug her nails into the lion skin, swinging herself onto his back. He rolled and she threw her fist into his side, making him jerk, but not much, and she hissed. She needed to get under his impenetrable cloak. He thrashed, trying to get her off his back but she clung on, grappling to reach the front of the lion skin and pull it from him. Every time she got purchase he pulled at her hand, ripping it from the material, and she roared in frustration. Power surged through her and she drew back her arm without thinking, then brought it crashing around into the side of his head.

For a second he went completely still and Lyssa's heart pounded so hard in her chest she thought it might give out. But then he began to thrash beneath her again, hard enough this time that her right hand was ripped from the cloak and she was thrown away from him. He spun so fast he was a blur and she didn't have time to avoid his massive fist. It caught her on her shoulder and she felt the bone snap.

Blinding pain cracked through the Rage and for a split second she couldn't move at all. Hercules's cold grey eyes shone as he drew his fist back again and Lyssa's skin fizzed to life, energy bursting through her body, her power beating back the pain. She kicked up, hard, and his swipe dragged through water beneath her. He followed, grabbing at her boot and pulling her back down towards him.

Letting him keep hold of her boot she ducked her head again, so that she was upside down and punched his stomach hard. Her fist hit the spot where the lion-skin cloak didn't quite meet and he shot backwards, his grip wrenching painfully at her foot before it was released. The look on his face was pure fury as he charged back towards her.

She couldn't beat him here. She couldn't move her arm at all and although she couldn't feel the pain, he was stronger than her. But she couldn't run either.

Rage flowed through her and she drew on it, remembering who she was. She was the granddaughter of Zeus, she had god-given strength. She was unbeatable.

Her muscles twitched and throbbed as she darted out of Hercules's path, but she wasn't fast enough. His hand caught her wounded shoulder and the pain roared back through her. He pulled her to him, gripping her throat with his other hand and squeezing. Madness danced in his grey eyes and fear enveloped Lyssa. She wasn't unbeatable. She was going to die. Her father would finish the job he had started four years ago.

She clawed frantically at his hand, scratching and pulling, kicking at him with her legs, but he was too strong. Black replaced the red in her vision and lancing pain throbbed through her head. She stared into Hercules's face, her body now refusing to answer her pleas to fight.

SUDDENLY HERCULES'S FACE CHANGED, morphing into a mask of pain, and he dropped her. She kicked backwards frantically, gasping for breath. What had happened?

Hercules was looking down at a deep gash in his leg, and red blood was seeping into the water around him. Epizon was beneath Hercules, holding a fallen steel feather like a sword, fury in his face. Lyssa kicked out, pushing all her Rage, all her power, all her hatred, into the movement.

Her boot connected with the side of Hercules's head and he went flying through the water.

HERCULES

For a moment, Hercules could see nothing but black, nausea roiling in his stomach as he spiralled through the water. He forced out the pain as he waved his arms, slowing his movement, his vision slowly clearing.

He had nearly done it. He had nearly ended the girl's miserable life. He'd been so close.

Something shot past him, fast, and he looked up. The birds. There were so many of them, swarming above him, beating their wings and sending razor sharp feathers down through the water towards him. Another whizzed past and he swore silently. He looked back to Lyssa, and his head pounded as he moved it. Her first mate was helping her swim back towards the volcano. It looked like her right arm was injured. *Excellent*, he thought.

He tested the use of his wounded leg. It stung as he moved it through the water but he could still swim well enough. He narrowed his focus to the red-haired girl and kicked towards her. This time he would strike where it would hurt her most.

LYSSA

L yssa's right arm was useless, and now that the Rage wasn't pulsing through her body so strongly, her muscles were twitching and spasming. It made swimming painfully slow.

Epizon pulled her towards the volcano, but although she didn't resist him, she didn't want to go back into the forge. *Up*, she thought, dizzily. She wanted to go up. She didn't want to be in the water any more, or in the suffocating heat of the forge. She needed air, space. Freedom.

She tugged against her first mate's grip and he looked back at her. She tipped her head back, looking towards the surface for the shadow of her ship. But there were so many birds. They ducked and swooped, their threatening motion clear. Come close and you'll die.

Lyssa and Epizon were out of range of their missiles but they couldn't get to the surface. There was little chance of her fighting and disabling two more now. They couldn't win and they were trapped.

Epizon suddenly pulled hard on her hand again, swerving her body though the water. She looked at him in confusion, then screamed as a shining feather slammed into his chest. Epizon's eyes widened as he soared backwards, but before Lyssa could reach him, Hercules was there, pulling the blade from Epizon's chest. Blood flowed from the wound, surrounding the two men, and the fear crippling Lyssa suddenly snapped, Rage-fuelled strength ripping through her aching body.

She kicked towards them, roaring, but Hercules was dragging Epizon up, towards the birds. Hercules looked back and launched the sharp feather at her. She dodged it easily, swimming fast after them, god-given power replacing pain and fear. Hercules had thrown the feather, she realised, pulling herself through the water with her left arm. He must have; the birds were too far away. And Epizon had pulled her out of the way. Her skin burned with white-hot anger. She needed to save him.

HERCULES HAD NEARLY REACHED the birds, pulling his lion skin up over his head as he came within range of their lethal feathers, and leaving a trail of Epizon's blood in his wake. Lyssa couldn't see if Epizon was conscious or not, and no matter how hard she kicked, she wasn't fast enough without the use of her right arm.

Missiles began to rain down and she spun and swerved to avoid them, her screams silent as feather after feather sailed past Epizon, some catching his limbs and spilling fresh blood into the water around him. Suddenly everything darkened, and for a brief moment the hail of feathers stopped. A massive shadow had moved over the surface of the water.

Hercules paused to look up but Lyssa kept moving, reaching for Epizon. The birds above suddenly scattered and Lyssa's breath caught as Nestor powered through the swarm, her great horse legs seeming to gallop through the water. She loosed her hammer at Hercules with an obvious roar, and the huge man hunched down inside his impenetrable cloak.

The distraction was all Lyssa needed. She grabbed Epizon's arm and pulled him from Hercules's grasp, kicking desperately up through the gap the centaur had cleaved, towards the surface.

Dragging Epizon's dead weight with one arm, her legs burning, she kicked desperately, but barely managed to move. Then Phyleus was on the other side of her, his cheeks puffed out with held breath. He grabbed Epizon's other arm with both of his and suddenly she was able to move again. They swam quickly, but Nestor kicked past them, her strong legs moving her at twice their speed. In seconds Lyssa's head broke the surface of the water, her heart swelling at the sight of the *Alastor* on the ocean beside her. Len was standing in the open cargo hauler on the side of the ship, just a foot above the waves, and Phyleus pulled himself up quickly. Together they heaved Epizon into the hauler, and Len got to work at once, tending the wound in his shoulder. Phyleus leaned over and grabbed for Lyssa's good arm, pulling her from the ocean.

'Is he OK?' she asked, staring down at Epizon's closed eyes.

'I don't know,' said Len calmly. 'This may have punctured his lung. We need to get him to the infirmary.'

'Captain,' called a voice. Lyssa turned to see Nestor, bobbing in the water behind them. 'I can't get out,' the centaur said, her face a mask of anger. Along with Phyleus, Lyssa stood up, the world tilting slightly as she did so, and they grabbed awkwardly at Nestor's front haunches. A well-timed wave swept the centaur forwards and she got enough purchase to scrabble into the hauler, knocking Lyssa's shoulder as she did so. Pain crashed through Lyssa's arm and chest and she cried out.

'Are you...'

She didn't hear Phyleus finish the question as she crumpled to the ground, darkness overtaking her.

18

EVADNE

Evadne was exhausted. After he'd rounded the volcano the telkhine had started swimming up the sheer side, swiftly and easily. She had followed, but now, most of the way up the volcano, her legs were aching from swimming and her shallow breathing was making her dizzy.

She slowed until she was at a complete stop, her eyes still fixed on the creature ahead. Her knees bumped against the rock as she drew her legs up, trying to stretch them. She forced herself to take a deep breath, panic rising in her as she did so. But, like last time, it was fine. Cool air filled her lungs. *See, you can breathe normally*, she scolded herself. She watched, grateful for the rest, as the telkhine crested the wide crater at the top of the volcano. What was up there?

With a slightly less reluctant breath she pushed off the rock and swam after it.

The lip of the crater was jagged, and completely vertical.

Evadne gripped it and pulled herself up slowly, not sure what to expect.

Her mouth fell open as she took in the view. A ring of steam jets circled the perimeter of the crater, but in the centre, cresting a tall thin black spire, was a bird's nest. It was about the size of a bed and there were four gleaming eggs in it, red, purple, white and blue. She pulled herself up a little further, saw movement on the other side of the crater, and ducked back down again quickly.

It was the telkhine. No, more than one. She shuffled along the rim of the crater, trying to get a better view through the steam. There were five or six of them, all with their backs to her. What were they doing?

Evadne swam up, considering the jets of steam. They weren't shooting out of the volcano constantly. Every now and then there was a pause. She watched the two jets closest to her carefully, counting in her head and praying there was a pattern.

After a few minutes she was certain there was. The bursts were separated by four seconds, and the pause lasted for three. She positioned herself as close to the steam as she could without the water scalding her skin, and waited. Four seconds after the first one stopped, she felt the water cool around her and then the steam cleared.

She swam as fast as she could through the gap, holding her breath. Heat engulfed her foot, but she pushed on, kicking hard, until she was through. She looked around quickly, expecting something to be guarding the eggs, but nothing happened. They were just there, in the middle of a tangle of metal wires and pipes.

None of the telkhines on the other side turned to her. Did they even know she was there? She swam towards them, curiosity burning. What were they looking at?

She swam slowly and carefully, doing her best to creep while under water, moving higher, hoping to be able to see them better from above. As she neared the steam she could see that there were six of them, and the central four were wearing iron crowns and holding ornately decorated hammers. She looked out in the direction they were all staring. The flock of stymphalian birds were just below, and Evadne couldn't see through them to the ocean floor, or to Hercules.

One of the telkhines lifted his hammer and four metal birds beat their wings towards him. Evadne backed up quickly, but the telkhine thrust the hammer out and the birds rushed in the direction he'd indicated. She frowned. All the telkhines were moving their hammers, even if only subtly, she realised. Were they controlling the birds with them? She watched, transfixed, as they flicked their wrists and small groups of stymphalian birds responded, moving in the water and firing their sharp feathers. They *were* controlling them, she was sure of it. If she could remove just one of these creatures...

HER HAND WENT to her hip and she pulled her slingshot from her belt. It was a risk. She would give her position away, for sure, and the tridents held by the two telkhines on either end of the line looked dangerous. But if she could just knock out one telkhine, her crew could win. The telkhines must be controlling at least three birds each; there were scores of them down there. All Hercules would have to do was destroy the immobile birds.

What if one of the other heroes got to them first? She might accidentally hand the win to somebody else. No,

Hercules would be in the thick of it, she had no doubt. His impervious lion skin and endless self-confidence would keep him closer to the beasts than any of the other heroes. She loaded a lead ball into her slingshot, aimed carefully through the steam, and fired.

19

HEDONE

edone hovered near the entrance to the lava tube, watching transfixed. There was no way Theseus would win this Trial, she thought, with no remorse or regret at the realisation. Lyssa and her crew were no longer in the running, Hercules had made sure of that. Hedone had thought her heart would stop when she and Theseus had emerged from the volcano just in time to see Lyssa kick Hercules in the head. But he'd shown her who was stronger. Hedone didn't know why he had thrown the feather at Epizon, but it had worked. Lyssa had stopped fighting and run, surely breaking all the rules when her ship landed on the water and her crew dived in to rescue her.

THE TRIAL WAS between Hercules and the giants now, with Theseus's trident-throwing below her getting him nowhere. Hercules had managed to disable one of the birds, his lion-skin cloak allowing him to get right underneath it, then grip its neck and twist. The giants had a huge metal net and although they already had two thrashing stymphalian birds secured in it, they didn't seem able to catch another one. They were using the net as a shield to get close to the flock but they couldn't open it to use it without losing the birds they had already snared.

WITHOUT WARNING a body tumbled past Hedone in the water and she gasped soundlessly, pressing herself flat against the volcano wall. It was a telkhine, wearing a weird metal crown. It looked like it was dead, or unconscious. It hit the ocean floor, causing a puff of moss and tiny creatures to erupt around it.

Hedone looked up where it had fallen from, and immediately noticed something odd in the swarm of metal birds. Lots of them had stopped moving. Completely. She looked to Hercules, who had clearly noticed it too. He moved like lightning, ripping the heads from two of the creatures before she could even draw a full breath. Everything around her shimmered slightly, then with a flash of light she was on the deck of the *Virtus*, her wet hair clinging to her face.

He had done it. Hercules had won.

THANK YOU

Thank you for reading Skies of Olympus, I hope you enjoyed it! It would mean so much to me if you could leave a review on Amazon, just a few words can help so much! You can do that here.

If you want to find out what happened when Lyssa and her crew went to Leo to pick up Tenebrae then you can read the exclusive short story, Winds of Olympus, by signing up for my newsletter here. You'll also be the first to know about new releases!

And you can carry straight on to book 3: Storms of Olympus!

Made in the USA
Columbia, SC
18 June 2021